Hooked On You

A Hatteras Island Novel

Jan Dawson

Library of Congress Control Number: 2023923643

ISBN 979-8-218-33906-7
Ebook ISBN 979-8-218-33907-4

Praise for Storm Season

Praise for "Storm Season"

"A beautiful romance set against the magical beauty of Hatteras Island. Jan masterfully weaves a tale of a tumultuous lost love that sweeps readers out to a breathtaking sea."

Donna Hayes, Producer, WGHP-TV, Greensboro-High Point

"When it seems the world has gone mad and everyone is reading post-apocalyptic horror stories or romance novels where no one treats anyone well, Jan's book is a breath of fresh air! Set on Hatteras Island, the novel takes a look at the daily lives of local residents and includes two different hurricanes, year apart. For a first novel, the characters and plot are both nicely developed and the story grabs you from the first chapter. A nice glimpse into life on Hatteras for visitors and a fun read for locals who will recognize many landmarks and storm prep procedures. A best seller from the beginning!"

Gee Gee Rossell, Owner, Buxton Village Books

"The perfect beach read! I took "Storm Season" on my week-long beach trip only to find myself zipping through all of it in two days--I couldn't put it down! The perfect page-turner for any book worm with a passion for love stories and the Carolina coast!"

Jeremy Spearman, Producer, WRAL-TV, Raleigh

A book needs three things to become a best-seller at Downtown Books: An Outer Banks setting, characters you'd love to spend a day on the beach with and a tale that keeps you in your beach chair from start to finish. Storm Season is all this and more! Set on Hatteras, Jan Dawson tells the story of three generations of women, a family-owned hotel, a hurricane and the man from the past who arrives with it and turns everyone's lives upside down. Jan is definitely a new OBX author to watch!

Jamie Anderson, Owner, Downtown Books, Manteo, NC and Duck's Cottage Books, Duck, NC

"*Storm Season* is a fun "second chance at love" romance! I devoured it in one sitting. Jan evokes the feel of Hatteras Island life, past and present, and delivers a happy but entirely realistic ending. An impressive debut!"

Susan Sawin, Owner, Island Bookstores, Duck and Corolla, NC

"Jan truly captures the essence of life on Hatteras Island like only a seasoned resident can. Storm Season captures the flavor of this wonderfully unique place through a story that explores the complications of family and the joys of love reclaimed."

Jenna Gunn, Best Selling Steamy Romance Author

For Dad, Uncle Ron and Uncle Rich
Three intrepid Hatteras anglers, casting for, and surely
catching, the big ones in heaven.

About Hooked On You

About the Book

Fishing. For fish or for men. She really didn't want to be involved with either one.

It was supposed to be a long weekend of rest, reading, and forgetting. Her heart was still heavy from her recent divorce, and she longed to get lost in books and the occasional bottle of wine. But then those plans quickly changed, and she realized that she would have to face her feelings of insecurity and failure in the most unusual circumstances.

Jenni wasn't ready for another man. But when she's thrown into a fishing tournament while visiting a friend, she finds there are plenty of men out there angling for more than just a fish. And it seems one man has his hook baited for her. Why does she do so many foolish things around him when she just wants to disappear?

Struggling to learn how to fish while at the same time keeping an eye on the too-good-to-be-true fisherman Caleb, Jenni is surprised by her conflicting feelings of wanting to be alone but yearning for new love. When their paths seem to continually cross in unexpected ways, she feels herself being reeled in. Is she really ready for another relationship or is Caleb the catch she shouldn't keep?

Hooked on You is a stand-alone sweet romance novel that brings back some of the favorite characters from *Storm Season*. If you enjoy stories about finding a new love, overcoming fears of trying something new, and laughing at oneself in spite of it all, you'll love this look at what it takes to catch the big one.

Chapter One

Jenni held her breath as the bridge approached. She was so close now.

The air left her at last when she crested the top of the new bridge and began the sloping descent to Pea Island, the name for the north end of Hatteras Island. She allowed herself to slow down and take in the view over Oregon Inlet. Thank God she was here, even if the pain she was feeling inside didn't match the beauty outside the window.

It was a beautiful April afternoon, the sun creating diamonds on the surface of the water. The old Coast Guard station was like a postcard in the afternoon sun.

She managed to laugh at herself for holding her breath as she drove up and then over the highest point of the new bridge. It was a holdover from her childhood when her family traversed the old bridge which was much steeper and narrower. She and her brothers and sisters would hold their breath as their dad drove them across that arch, seeing who could make it the longest.

Back then, she had dreams of the woman she would become. She saw someone who had self-confidence and achieved great things. She would be carefree and happy. She was sure of those things back then.

With those thoughts, tears came to her eyes, threatening to spill down her cheeks.

But now she was on Hatteras Island and with that exhale she relaxed. It was going to be a wonderful weekend.

It had to be.

She needed this long weekend to try to finally put the past year behind her. The separation and divorce from Compton Lee Satterwaite III, or Compy, had exhausted her and changed her in ways she was ashamed to admit.

They'd been married five years. In the past year, she'd spent too many hours beating herself up for everything she had or had not done to make the marriage work.

Despite family and friends sharing that they'd had misgivings from the first—why didn't they share those thoughts with her a long time ago? Logically, she knew that both parties in any divorce had to share blame, but she convinced herself it was all her fault.

She moved back home to Raleigh, found a position in financial development at a non-profit she had always admired, and promptly, as her best friend Caitlin said, fell off the face of the earth.

It was Caitlin who begged her to take this long weekend

to come to Hatteras, to stay at her mom's beach house in Frisco, and to have some long overdue heart-to-heart talks over a bottle of wine.

Jenni suddenly banged her fist on the steering wheel.

She was supposed to text Caitlin at Whalebone Junction to let her know she was a little over an hour away.

Caitlin's mom, Barb Thomas, was an excellent cook, but she was a stickler for wanting everyone to be present the minute food came off the stove or out of the oven. She declared that for each minute it sat on the table, some of the flavor disappeared, and she wouldn't be blamed.

Jenni glanced in the rearview mirror to see if there was much traffic. She thought she'd just slow down and gently pull off to the side, being careful to keep two tires on the pavement and out of the sand.

Just as she started to pull over, a large truck, which must have been in her blind spot, came barreling by and caught her totally by surprise.

She jerked the steering wheel and groaned inwardly as she felt the two wheels on the left leave Highway 12 and settle unhappily in the sand.

This can't be, it just can't. She shook her head. *Compy would assume I would do something like this. I...*

She forcefully stopped that train of thought.

It didn't matter any longer what Compy thought or didn't think.

At this moment, she had to figure out a way to get unstuck.

She'd read somewhere that floor mats were a good solution for tire traction, and she was about to get out of the car and begin the process of trying to extricate herself from the situation when a vehicle slowed down, coming up beside her.

Her spirit sank when she realized it was a large pickup with more fishing rods than she'd ever seen in her life.

A window rolled down and music, loud music, assaulted her ears.

She could see four guys in the truck. The driver was motioning to the guy next to him to turn the music down.

"Hey there, looks like you are going to need a tow," the driver said as he leaned across the passenger in the front seat who was guzzling down a beer. "Want some help?"

Jenni's knee-jerk response was to say, "*What do you think?*" but she held her tongue and said, "No thanks, I think I can handle this. I stopped to send a text and a truck came by and I was startled and..."

Her cheeks burned, and she wished they'd drive on.

But the driver just said, "You really don't want to get yourself in any deeper, and a tow truck would cost a small fortune. Hang on, and we'll get you out."

Jenni shrugged and nodded. She thought she heard a few crass comments coming from the guys in the truck, but it was already positioning itself in front of her.

The driver hopped out and reached into his truck bed, pulling out a sturdy rope. He walked over to the car and grinned.

"When you travel down here, it's always a good idea to be prepared. You know you shouldn't pull off the side of the road along here. I'm Caleb, by the way," he said all in one breath.

Jenni looked at him and felt at that moment that next to Compy, she'd never seen such a handsome man. Then she realized he was still talking.

"...and I'll attach this rope to something sturdy on the front of your little car, and then when I get back to the truck, you start the ignition and put it in neutral, and we'll get you right out. Are you here for the big fishing tournament?"

It took a moment for Jenni to realize he'd asked a question unrelated to her current predicament.

"God, no." She almost shuddered. "I'm the last person on earth you'd find at a fishing tournament."

"Huh." He shrugged. "Me and the boys never miss this one. It's called the "Hook, Line, and Sinker" tournament, and it's a big one. So, why are you here?"

She stiffened a bit at his incessant questioning, but she realized he was helping her out, so she decided to be as polite, but as brief, as she could. "I'm just spending some time with my college roommate. You know, a girls' weekend. Books, wine, that sort of thing."

She was interrupted by a voice from inside the truck, "Come on, Romeo. We've got shrimp baskets waiting for us for dinner if we ever get there."

Raucous laughter followed.

"Ignore them." Caleb grinned. "They've already started in on the beer, and they're ready for their guys' weekend, I guess you'd call it."

Jenni looked at him. Had he started too?

As if reading her mind, he quickly added, "Not me. I don't drink and drive."

Jenni nodded and placed her hands firmly on the steering wheel. "Well, let's see if you can get me out. What do I owe you?"

Caleb shook his head. "You don't owe me anything." Then he cocked his head to the right. "Well, maybe just the pleasure of knowing your name."

"Ah, I'm Jenni, and thanks for this. It was very nice of you. Good luck with your tournament and all."

"OK, Jenni." Caleb grinned again. "You know, just a

few miles away there's a parking lot at the Pea Island Visitor's Center. You can park there and send your text or whatever."

Caleb jumped back in the truck and signaled out the window for her to start her ignition.

She placed the car in neutral and felt the tug of the rope. Then slowly, she was moving, and in a matter of seconds, she was back on the highway.

Thankfully, there was very little traffic as Caleb re-emerged to undo the rope. He turned and waved slightly, got back into the truck, and headed on down the road, fishing rods saluting her as he departed.

Chapter Two

She put her car in gear and headed out as well, her heart beating just a bit too fast for her liking.

She never believed those stories of instant attraction but along with her racing heart, her palms were sweaty, and her mouth was dry.

She knew she was attracted to this "hero" who'd just saved her time and probably several hundred dollars, but she also knew men couldn't be trusted; not in matters of love, anyway.

But maybe she should give him the benefit of the doubt

about giving directions, because, just as he had said, the Pea Island Visitor's Station was just a few minutes south.

She pulled in and grabbed her phone to text Caitlin.

Hey! I'm at Pea Island. Bit of an adventure but it's all good. I'll be there in about 45.

Caitlin must have been waiting for her text, knowing what time Jenni had left and what time she should arrive.

Been wondering where you were, girl! Mom has her seafood lasagna ready to pop in the oven. I've got some news for you. See you soon!

Jenni got back on the highway and settled in for the rest of the drive. Once again, she noted the beauty of this early spring afternoon.

There were still a few migrating birds about, and the angle of the sun made everything look a bit softer than during the heat of the summer. The sea oats were green and eager to begin their season, gently swaying in the breeze.

Her thoughts eventually drifted back to what had just happened. She knew she was fortunate to have someone pull her out in such a short period of time.

If Compy had been in that truck, he'd have sounded the horn and laughed, but he never would have stopped to help. She was sure of that.

But Caleb had stopped. He had been nothing but sympathetic and nice and helpful.

She would never use those adjectives with Compy.

Her face felt flushed and when she brushed her hair from her forehead, her brow was wet.

She reflected again on her good fortune.

It was broad daylight now, but in a few hours, she would have been stuck in the approaching darkness. That would have been worse.

She was thankful her boss, Dee, had told her to go ahead and leave around lunchtime. Traffic had been easy coming from Raleigh, but with her little escapade added on, it was almost 5:30.

Her mind kept drifting back to Caleb.

He seemed so nice, so selfless. But *there are no nice guys anymore. If Compy taught me anything, it's not to trust anyone.*

She was certain Caleb and his buddies were thinking she was a total idiot for pulling off into the sand.

It wasn't a great way to start the trip. She sincerely hoped things would improve moving forward.

She turned her attention to happier thoughts.

I wonder what Caitlin's surprise is. Maybe she and Andrew are finally getting engaged!

After graduation, while Jenni had stayed in Columbia, Caitlin had moved to Charleston and continued her studies in nursing at the Medical University. She'd met Andrew there and they'd been dating for what seemed to Jenni to be forever.

Probably a wise move on her part, she acknowledged. *If only I had…*

She made herself stop that train of thought which always led to self-recrimination and more hurt. Instead, she focused on her surroundings.

Even though she'd read about them, she was surprised to cross two more new bridges on her way down the island. How many years had it been since she'd been here? At least eight or ten, she reasoned. Too long.

The ocean always had a calming influence on her, and even though she planned to hole up at the "Mermaid Mansion," Caitlin's mom's beach house, for the better part of this visit, she was sure she'd take at least one beach walk.

She hadn't checked the weather forecast, but if it was going to be as nice as it was today, a walk would really be in order.

A walk with Caleb, perhaps?

Stop that! She hit her hand on her thigh.

She had no business thinking about him or any other man.

She thought about the possibilities of Caitlin's good news.

She was surprised when she reached Buxton and headed on to Frisco.

As she pulled into the driveway of the house, she could see Caitlin waving from the porch.

Like all the houses in this little development, the "Mansion" was up on pilings.

Caitlin bounded down the front steps to greet her with hugs as she stopped the car and stepped out.

"It's so great you're here," Caitlin exclaimed. "Look at you, you're nothing but skin and bones. Wait until Mom sees you."

Jenni's face heated up again.

They called it the divorce diet, and in the past year, she'd not only lost interest in the world around her but in food as well.

She knew that since Caitlin had last seen her, she had lost probably twenty pounds, pounds she really didn't need to lose.

They had both played tennis at the University of South Carolina and had always been in good shape.

"I guess I just don't eat much anymore," Jenni admitted. "But I can assure you that your mom's cooking will no doubt entice me. And I am starving."

Caitlin gave her friend a knowing look. "I realize this

past year has been hard for you, but you've got to start living again. Where's my old Jenni?"

When Jenni didn't answer, and just looked at the horizon, Caitlin quickly retreated. "I'm sorry. I know I'm pushy. Let's get your stuff upstairs and get ready to eat. I'm anxious to hear about the crazy adventure you mentioned."

"And the surprise?" Jenni asked.

"After dinner," said Caitlin as she grabbed one of Jenni's bags and headed up the steps. "Come on. Time for a glass of wine before dinner."

Barb Thomas met them at the door and gave Jenni another huge hug. "It's so good to see you, Jenni," she exclaimed. "My word, you're thin. I'm so sorry about, well, about what happened, but I am glad you're here now. Caitlin has been counting the hours."

"Thanks, Miss Barb," Jenni said as she took a deep breath returning the hug. "It has been rough for sure, but I'm working on things."

Barb stepped aside, and Jenni saw a woman who looked a lot like Barb, just a bit older.

"Jenni, this is my sister, May Ellen Randall. She's here for the weekend as well."

Jenni reached out to shake May Ellen's hand and wondered what had precipitated her visit here at the same time. "It's a pleasure to meet you, Mrs. Randall."

"Please, just call me May Ellen. And it's time you started calling Barb by her first name. None of that Miss Barb stuff. Makes us feel ancient," May Ellen said, winking at Barb.

"It's just so hard for me to make that change," admitted Jenni, laughing. "Upbringing and all, I guess. But I'll try."

True to form, dinner was ready in a few minutes, and Jenni and Caitlin moved from the porch, where they'd been enjoying a glass of wine while looking at the sound, to the dining room table.

Jenni thought she'd never tasted anything as good as Barb's lasagna and was happily lost in a food reverie when Caitlin asked her about her "adventure" on the drive down.

After asking for a second glass of wine, Jenni began to tell them about getting stuck in the sand.

"You are so lucky that you didn't have to call a tow," Caitlin exclaimed. "That's really expensive. But more importantly, tell us more about your knight in shining armor."

"Well, I think his shining armor was a Ford F-150, but I honestly can't tell you anything about him," Jenni replied, pushing a stray bit of noodle around on her plate. "He was OK, I guess."

"Hmmm." Caitlin looked carefully at Jenni. "I know you really well, and I just get the feeling you're not telling us everything."

"Not much to tell, honestly." Jenni looked up. "He and his buddies are here for some sort of big deal fishing tournament."

She noticed that glances were being exchanged among the three other women in the room, and Caitlin took a large gulp of wine before looking directly back at Jenni.

"Yes, well, about that tournament," she began. "You see, I knew it was going on this weekend, but I figured it would be OK because while Mom, Aunt May Ellen, Aunt Liz, and I were fishing, you could just relax here at the house. Then we could regale you with our fishing tales when we got home."

"But..." said Jenni slowly, noting that Aunt Liz apparently was not in the house. "What?"

Caitlin grinned sheepishly. "My Aunt Liz, Mom's other

sister, has Covid, and so there was no way she could make the trip. Mom just found out yesterday. So, we thought you could be our fourth angler. We have to have four." Caitlin tried to finish with a positive flourish. "And that's my surprise!"

Jenni sat in stunned silence.

What happened to Andrew and the ring? She knew that good manners meant she needed to say something and that as a guest that should be something in the affirmative, but at that moment, nothing positive would come out. All she could manage was, "Y'all are joking, right?"

Barb and May Ellen said nothing.

Caitlin started to respond, but Jenni interrupted.

"Come on, Caitlin, seriously. You can't mean that. I have never fished in my life. I don't like the thought of fishing, and I know absolutely nothing about it. This is a big tournament, according to Caleb of the Ford F-150, and so I should definitely *not* be participating."

Barb sighed audibly and, as if by a secret sister code, she and May Ellen both began clearing up dishes and headed into the kitchen.

Jenni thought about her stack of unread books and the nice bottles of wine she'd brought. She thought about reading under a blanket and watching the gulls and pelicans soar over the sound. She thought about trying to forget about Compy and rebuilding her self-esteem.

Surely, putting a line in the ocean wasn't going to help her do that.

Then she glanced at Caitlin who was looking at her expectantly.

"I can teach you," her friend blurted out. "You know I can fish. I've been doing it forever. So have Mom and Aunt May Ellen. We can show you what to do, and tomorrow, we can practice. It's Wednesday, and the tournament doesn't start until Friday morning. We'd fish Friday and half a day Saturday and then there's a banquet Saturday night. I mean, you can read when we come home. It'll be fun."

When Jenni continued to just look at her friend, Caitlin scrunched up her eyes as only she could do. "Please, please, please."

Jenni was exasperated. But she also knew that she couldn't stay here and let her hostess and family down. Clearly, since yesterday, they were counting on her, assuming she'd go along. They obviously had no idea that Jenni knew less than zero about fishing. And that trying to teach her would be an exercise in futility.

But in her heart, Jenni knew she couldn't say no after all.

"OK, Caitlin," she said. "But this will be a disaster, and I hope you don't think you'll ever succeed. Compy would assure you if there's a way to screw it up, I will."

Caitlin's eyes flared. "But he isn't here, and he's not a part of your life. Get him out of your head!" Then she walked around the table and put her arms around her friend. "You can do this, it's not hard. And maybe this will help get your mind off him. Lord knows, something has to do that."

Jenni glanced up and saw Barb and May Ellen emerge from the kitchen.

"Honey, I know this isn't how you'd hoped to spend your weekend, but we'll make it fun for you, I promise," said Barb. "And I'm really grateful. Liz felt awful that we might have to scratch. You don't have to worry about the entry fee since it's already covered, and I've got plenty of rods and such. Caitlin can take you to the tackle shop in the morning, and in the afternoon, you can try a bit of fishing."

Jenni knew her true ignorance was about to show. "Tackle shop?" she queried. "What will I need to get there?"

"Well," May Ellen interjected. "I suspect you didn't bring any waders with you, so a pair of those will come in handy. And a pair of gloves and maybe a cap too. We all want to be really fashionable. We'll look the part even if we don't catch a thing."

Jenni looked at the three of them and saw they were smiling.

"And don't you worry about the cost," Barb was saying with her hands firmly on her hips, meaning there was no room for debate. "We dragged you into this, so we will outfit you accordingly." And with that, she and May Ellen retreated through the swinging doors into the kitchen, leaving Caitlin and Jenni at the table.

"Look at it this way," Caitlin said while draining the last of her glass. "You'll be so busy trying to figure out what's going on, you won't have time to think of old what's-his-name."

Jenni just nodded and joined her in picking up the last of the dishes and carrying them into the kitchen.

At the doorway, she paused and looked at her friend. Her eyes were laughing but she tried to muster a serious tone.

"I'm doing this for all of you, particularly your mom and your aunt. But you owe me, CayCay," Jenni warned, using her pet name for her old roommate. "You owe me big time. And there will be nothing, I repeat, nothing on social about me at this tournament. No Instas, no nothing. Good grief. Waders..."

Chapter Three

Jenni woke up to the smell of bacon and coffee, her two most favorite food items in the world.

She was confused at first, thinking she was still at home in her apartment, but then the reality of her situation came flooding back, and she felt a knot form in the pit of her stomach.

She should have just politely said no to Caitlin and her mom and aunt. But then what? Would she have felt comfortable lounging around, reading with a wine glass in her hand while they missed out on something that was so clearly special to them?

Obviously, the answer to that was no. So, she rolled out of bed, grabbed a pair of leggings and a t-shirt, and made her way to the kitchen following the breakfast aromas.

"Aha, so there you are, sleeping beauty." Barb laughed as she handed her a mug of steaming coffee. "As I recall from Caitlin, you take it black, right?"

Jenni nodded happily as she took a sip. "And I know, Miss Barb, I mean Barb, that you and Caitlin could never understand that. But my parents both drink it black, and so I do too. Makes it pretty easy wherever I go." She paused and glanced around the kitchen. "Where are Caitlin and May Ellen?"

"Well, Caitlin already had her breakfast, and she's in the shower. May Ellen got up at first light and went out for a walk on the beach. I'm sure she'll be back shortly. She loves to go shelling. She also likes solitude, she says. We sisters need our space." And Barb laughed again.

"What time is it?" asked Jenni, suddenly feeling as though she'd seriously overslept.

"Just a few minutes after eight," Barb responded. "By this time tomorrow, we'll be busy fishing!"

"We will?" Jenni's heart sank. "Um, what time will we get up and all?"

"The tournament starts at seven, so we'll be sure to have our gear all set tonight as best we can, and that way, we can head out about 6:30, depending on where we'll be fishing." Barb set down a plate of bacon, eggs, and toast in front of Jenni. "I know you probably feast on yogurt every morning, but for these few days, I want you to just enjoy my cooking."

Jenni looked at the plate and realized how long it had been since she'd had a full breakfast. "I will." She nodded in earnest. "So, can you kind of run me through what tomorrow will be like?"

Barb grabbed her coffee and pulled up a chair at the table next to Jenni. "The first thing is today, around two, I'll go to the captains' meeting. We'll go over all the rules and such, and then we'll draw for positions."

"You mean, we don't get to fish just wherever?"

Barb shook her head. "Now, that would be a mess because everyone would want to be at the Point. So, no, you draw positions. Volunteers will be out on the beaches today marking the spots. We'll fish one spot tomorrow morning, that's basically seven until eleven-thirty. Then from twelve-thirty until five, we have another spot, and Saturday morning a third spot.

Jenni was shaking her head. "I had no idea. It seems like a lot of moving around, but I suppose it makes it a bit fairer that way."

"It does," agreed Barb. "And we won't really stop somewhere for lunch tomorrow. We'll just pack up and move. I'll have sandwiches and stuff in the truck so we can eat and fish at the same time."

Jenni thought about bait and lunch, and suddenly, she lost her appetite. "I'm kind of really nervous about all of this. Are stations close together? Will other people see me?"

"Afraid so, dear. Everyone spreads out in their allotted area, and so you pretty much are right there with your next-door neighbors on either side. Since you are new to casting, we'll try to put you at an end with no one next to you. Wouldn't want you to get into a tangle."

Jenni groaned inwardly. She could see it now, her line entwined with Caleb's and everyone having a big laugh as she made a fool of herself in front of him yet again.

But where did that thought come from? Why would she think about him when she had so many other things to think about getting ready for the tournament?

She was beginning to realize how solitary her life had become in the past year. Was she that desperate for attention?

Caleb was just someone she met in passing. She shouldn't allow herself to keep thinking about him.

She brought her attention back to Barb who was discussing the specifics.

"Our team is called the 'Reel Southern Ladies.'" She smiled. "Get it – R-E-E-L."

Jenni laughed. She had to admit Barb looked really into this and seemed to be enjoying teaching Jenni the fundamentals.

"Now, there are all kinds of tournaments here during the year." Barb took a sip of her coffee. "What I'm telling you only pertains to this one. You will have to do everything yourself – that means redoing your rig if you lose one, putting on your bait, and taking your fish off the hook. We use cut bait, usually bloodworms, mullet, and shrimp."

Jenni pushed her plate away. Suddenly, breakfast had lost a bit of its appeal.

Barb stopped and looked at her. "I know that this has probably upset your apple cart, honey, but when you're out there in the wind and whatnot, you don't think about it as much."

"Alright." Jenni nodded once. "I'll just deal with it."

"Great," said Barb, picking up where she left off. "When you catch something, we'll put it in a bucket until the judges arrive. They'll measure it. You get a point for any fish over what the minimum is for that species. Then you throw the fish back because this tournament is all catch and release."

Jenni mulled that over for a moment. "But what if you catch a really big one? And it's too big for the bucket?"

"Well, I'd love that." Barb chuckled. "The judges are responsible for five or six stations, so they're usually nearby, but you could call them if you felt it was urgent. Then they would come over and measure right away so that you can get the fish back in the ocean."

Jenni started to ask another question, but Barb was on a roll and just continued, "In April, we are mainly fishing for puppy drum, but it's also possible we'll see some sea mullet, trout, flounder, and maybe some blues. And if you catch a trash fish, they don't count."

"I hate to be so ignorant, but I have to ask, what's a trash fish?"

"Rays, blow toads, or puffer fish, sharks, those kinds of things." Barb set her hands on the table.

Jenni stood up and got a refill of her coffee. She had so much to learn in such a short period of time. It was like cramming for an exam back in college.

"We're all women," she stated. "Is that unusual?"

"Not hardly. I'd say about twenty-five or thirty percent of teams in tournaments are all women. In this tournament, all teams compete on the same footing, all men's teams, women's, and mixed. But like I said, all tournaments are slightly different. I like this one 'cause we're all competing against each other."

"Last question, I promise." Jenni smiled as she sat back down. "Have the fish been biting?"

"Good question." Barb finished her coffee and stood up to move to the sink. "It's been so-so recently, but with the weather turning tomorrow, things might improve. Could be a bit 'drummy' as they say. Bad weather brings the drum fish."

"That's right," said Caitlin as she walked into the kitchen. "Which means, my dear Jenni, we will also need to get you a warmer shirt or something for tomorrow. Which also means, you need to get showered, and we'll get this day started."

Jenni pushed back her chair and saluted Caitlin as she walked by. "I can be ready in less than a half hour. Let's get this show on the road."

The front door opened, and May Ellen greeted them with a handful of shells. "It was a great morning." She smiled as she dropped the shells onto the table. Then she turned to Jenni. "Are you getting excited about tomorrow now?"

"I'm not sure what word I would use," she admitted. "But since I'm in, I need to get my lessons started."

May Ellen gave her a thumbs up, and Jenni disappeared down the hallway, re-emerging as promised just thirty minutes later. She and Caitlin hopped into Barb's truck as Barb indicated she'd take Caitlin's car to the captains' meeting that afternoon. A truck would be necessary on the beach if they intended to get any practice done that afternoon.

The tackle shop was just a few minutes away. Jenni's eyes widened as they drew closer to the parking lot.

"Lordy, this place looks like Walmart the day after Thanksgiving," exclaimed Jenni as Caitlin maneuvered into one of the few parking spaces. "What is everyone doing?"

Caitlin laughed. "Everyone needs a new rod or a new reel or the latest lure." She turned off the truck. "But honestly, I think everyone is trying to scope out the competition, listen for who's catching what where, and exchanging a few fish stories."

Jenni stopped for a moment to take it all in as they walked into the shop. There were rods of every size. Reels too. She also noticed colorful lures, some of them looking like Halloween decorations or maybe some sort of weird sea creature.

"Do we use those?" She pointed to one very bright display.

"No," Caitlin laughed. "Those are for offshore fishing. We'll get our bait for today's practice right as we leave. Let's get you some waders now, and a warm shirt, a hat, and some gloves."

The next several minutes were spent checking sizes, colors, and brands as Jenni remained fascinated with what seemed to be a parallel universe of anglers in a tournament-induced frenzy.

She decided on a pink and purple tassel cap, thinking she could at least add a bit of color to the olive drab of everything else.

For one brief moment, she thought she saw Caleb checking out at the register in the front of the store, but whoever he was disappeared, and she didn't see him again.

She was surprised at the hint of disappointment, but she replaced those feelings by concentrating on what was still to come in the day ahead.

Chapter Four

"Alrighty, what's next?" she asked Caitlin as they placed the packages on the back seat of the truck.

She had tried to pay for her new wardrobe, but Barb was adamant with Caitlin about picking up the costs. The only thing Jenni did pay for was her fishing license which everyone had forgotten she needed. Thankfully, Caitlin remembered when they saw someone else get one at the check-out.

"I feel like I've moved into some alternate world where everything revolves around fish," she commented to Caitlin as they pulled out onto Highway 12.

"It is a bit, I guess. Some people take it way too seriously, I think. It's supposed to be relaxing and a chance to just cast away your cares, so to speak. But tournaments are a whole different thing. So, the next thing we'll do is go out onto the beach and practice everything. I'll walk you through the steps of baiting and casting. Don't worry."

They turned off the highway and cruised through the campground area to what Jenni saw was a sign for Ramp 49. As Caitlin put the truck into 4-wheel drive, Jenni was amazed at how easily she navigated through the sand.

There were plenty of anglers already hard at work. It was hard to say how many of them would be in the tournament in the morning, but Jenni suspected a fair amount.

Surely, Caleb and his crew would be out there somewhere getting a feel for things. She hoped they wouldn't cross paths here at the beach.

It was another beautiful April day, and Jenni found it extremely hard to believe that the weather could change so much by tomorrow.

"Come on, let's get started," Caitlin said breezily as she parked the truck, hopped out, and went into the bed for the rods and some bait. "You'll definitely want to wear your gloves tomorrow, but for today, you can use your hands to bait the hook."

Jenni grimaced. "No, thanks, I'll learn with the gloves on since you say I'll need them tomorrow, and honestly..."

Caitlin laughed. "I know, you don't want to touch any bait. Well, just watch me now and do what I do."

For the next two hours, Caitlin took the time to show Jenni how to bait a hook, how to hold the rod, and finally how to cast. At first, Jenni felt awkward, and her baited hook plopped miserably just a few yards from where she stood.

"Don't try to heave it out there," coached Caitlin. "Hey, we played tennis. You know how the racket does the work. Same thing. Let the rod do the work. Nice and easy. Just don't ever forget to flip the bail. It's the thing that lets the line fly freely when you cast."

"And what happens if I don't?"

"You'll see your bait go flying such a long way, and you'll feel really good, until you realize your fishing line has snapped, and you've lost your entire rig."

"Oh. And then what? Can I quit fishing?"

"Um, that would be a no," stated Caitlin. "It would mean one of us would have to teach you how to put on a new one with the knots and all because we can't do it for you. In fact, since you mentioned it, let's do that now."

Jenni wanted to say there's no need. She'd remember to flip the bail. She wouldn't make a mistake like that, would she?

Regardless, for the next hour, she watched Caitlin and tried to do it on her own. Her frustration was reaching a high point when she finally succeeded.

"You go, girl!" Caitlin hollered. "I'll make you an angler yet!"

Jenni glanced around mortified. But no one seemed to notice. Everyone else on the beach anywhere near them was either actively fishing or grabbing a sandwich and a drink with their rod in a holder. They weren't paying a bit of attention to her.

But noticing the food made her intensely hungry again.

Caitlin must have noticed the same thing. She took out her phone and glanced at the time.

"Wow, we've been out here a while. Let's go grab a bite to eat at Marcie's, and then we can try again this afternoon."

It was clear that Marcie's was the spot for lunch. Even

though it was well past lunch hour, the parking lot was heaving, and Caitlin only found a spot because someone pulled out just as they drove up.

"Doesn't look so special from the outside." Jenni looked at the cedar shake building with the ramshackle porch and tilted sign that might have been hand-painted.

"Ah, looks are deceiving. I guess, years ago when you came, this wasn't here. But it is an institution now. And Marcie's shrimp baskets are to die for. You'll see."

There was a bit of a line even at that hour, so Jenni took it all in as they stepped inside.

She noticed a very attractive older woman, with bobbed blonde hair and a bright blue Marcie's t-shirt, smiling and chatting to guests as she gave orders to the kitchen and the servers. "Who's that?"

"That would be Marcie. She is something else."

"She's really pretty." Jenni scanned the menu.

"I heard she was Miss North Carolina once upon a time." Caitlin nodded. "She's got beauty and brains, and she's made a small fortune here, I'm guessing. But the thing is, she's got a personality to match."

By then, they had reached the head of the line, and Marcie motioned for them to have a seat while she bussed the table. "Well, Caitlin Thomas. How are you? Are you here for the tournament?" Marcie asked.

"Yep, glad to be back for this one. And this is my college roommate, believe it or not, Jenni Satterwaite—ah, I mean, Kirk," Caitlin stammered as she remembered Jenni had gone back to her maiden name. "Sorry, Jenni."

Jenni smiled warmly at Marcie. "It's very nice to meet you. I've been hearing so many good things about this place. Can't wait to try a shrimp basket."

"Make that two, please." Caitlin turned her head to the side a bit. "Hey, is that the Smiths I see over there?"

"Yep," said Marcie. "And SeaAnna and Mike are in town too. You know Mike's taken to offshore fishing in a big way, but I think they are here just for fun. Chris and Susan will be judging. And I believe Jo will be here for the weekend, coming over from Belhaven. Now, let me put your order in."

Marcie moved away, and Jenni looked at her friend. "How do you know all these people?"

"I come here pretty often, Jenni. I love it here, and so do Mom and Dad. And with them being on the island so often since they retired, they are in on all the local news, and they have made a lot of new friends."

After sipping the water that had been quickly placed on the table, Caitlin added, "Susan and Chris have an amazing story. They reconnected after more than forty years apart. And Mike and SeaAnna, Susan's daughter, have just started coming to the island. Their daughter, JoBell Leonard, is at the North Carolina Center for Aquatic Research in Belhaven."

"That name sounds familiar." Jenni could swear it. "I'm pretty sure I've read about JoBell Leonard in my alumni news."

"We'll go over and say hi before we leave and you can ask," Caitlin said as she watched the food coming to their table. "One thing about Marcie's, the service is really fast. Let's eat."

They were just finishing up when Caitlin saw the Smiths and the Leonards get up to leave. Caitlin caught Chris's eye with a wave, and the four came over to the table. Caitlin rose to give everyone hugs and then introduced Jenni as her former roommate, and an alum of St. Adrian's.

"Didn't your daughter go to St. Adrian's too?" Jenni asked SeaAnna.

"She did! What a coincidence. Are you here for the tournament this weekend?"

"I am now." Jenni laughed and explained the situation.

"For sure when Jo gets here, you'll have to meet her. She's coming tomorrow evening. I had hoped she would come earlier and maybe spend some time with her dad and Dare on his boat, but it didn't work out with her class schedule."

"Dare?"

"Dare Davis. He's a charter boat captain. And Jo's good friend, I guess you'd have to say. I really wish for more," SeaAnna's voice trailed off. Mike touched her shoulder and shook his head as if to say, "Not now."

Jenni glanced at Chris and Susan who seemed quick to change the direction the conversation had taken. Susan's smile lit up the room. "Well, they will be together at the banquet with us, so, Jenni, you can meet both of them then."

"For sure," Jenni agreed. "We'll let you go, then. We'll see you at the banquet."

"Oh, you may see us before then." Chris laughed; the awkward moment now gone. "Since Susan and I are volunteering as judges, maybe you'll catch the big one, and we'll have to measure." He winked at Jenni as they walked toward the exit.

"You never know what you might catch," said Caitlin to Jenni. "You just never know."

"Did I sense something about Jo and that Dare?"

"They've been together forever, and I guess SeaAnna would like to see them a bit more...committed, shall we say?" Caitlin smiled.

Jenni just nodded as they paid the bill and walked back into the parking lot.

In her mind, Jo would be smart to keep things just as they were, but who was she to judge? She, who had made so many mistakes in her marriage. Just because she no longer trusted anyone, didn't mean others shouldn't.

She was convinced that she was the reason everything went wrong in her marriage.

Plus, there were no good guys anymore. Too good to be true, as the old saying went.

Caleb, for example. He was surely in that category. He was handsome, thoughtful, and clearly, he knew his way around island life. What was missing? There had to be some fault, somewhere.

Banishing those distressing ruminations, she tried to look enthusiastic and said in her most positive voice, "I guess it's time to practice a bit more. If I'm going to hook the big one, you know? And I didn't know there was a banquet.

I mean, what? Do we dress up our waders?"

Caitlin turned the truck back toward the ramp access. "Look, I know this wasn't what you had planned, but it's going to be fun. Trust me." She smiled. "And, at any rate, it's a weekend we'll certainly never forget."

Chapter Five

When Jenni woke up, it wasn't to the smell of bacon and eggs, but to the sound of the wind howling. She rolled over to look out her window and saw the tree limbs swaying back and forth and a bit of spitting rain hitting the glass.

Ugh. I can't believe I have to get up and go out in that today. It's so warm and comfortable right here in bed.

She rolled back over hoping to get in a bit more sleep, but her phone alarm went off right on schedule. It was five-thirty.

She sat up and rubbed her eyes and threw her legs over the bed. The floor was much cooler to the touch, so she knew the temperature must have dropped a bit. She could hear the others stirring and knew they wanted to be on their way by six-thirty, so she stumbled into the bathroom and got the shower going.

When she walked into the kitchen, Barb was already busy making egg and sausage biscuits and packing a huge cooler. "Mornin', Jenni." She smiled. "Are you ready for your big debut?"

Jenni reached for the mug of coffee Barb handed her, took a sip, and attempted a smile. "I guess so. Caitlin really taught me a lot yesterday, but I am not sure how much of it I'll remember. It was a crash course in Tournament Fishing 101 for sure."

May Ellen and Caitlin walked in at the same time. It was very clear given the layers they were wearing they expected a very chilly day. May Ellen looked askance at Jenni's long-sleeved T-shirt. "You surely are going to put something over that, right?"

"Oh, sure." She had hoped that the T-shirt would be enough. The heavy plaid shirt they purchased at the tackle shop seemed a bit over the top when they bought it, but now, looking at the others, she realized she was definitely underdressed for the occasion.

"I just came in for my coffee. I'll go and put it on right now." She rose from the table. "Do you need my help packing up the truck?"

"No," Barb replied as she closed and fastened the lid of the cooler. "This is it. Glad we packed most everything up last night. Get yourself together and let's plan to leave in a few minutes. We're right on schedule."

Jenni pulled the tags off the shirt and tugged it over her head, adjusting the waders over the top of her jeans. She pulled her hair back in a ponytail and stuck her new tassel cap on her head. She stepped back and looked at herself in the mirror, not sure if she wanted to laugh or cry. Maybe both.

This was way out of her comfort zone.

Or was it? The old Jenni would have relished this new challenge. The current Jenni felt overwhelmed and at a loss.

She hoped she would at least not let the team down, even if she didn't add much to their efforts.

She ran into the bathroom one more time, not knowing what the proper toilet arrangements would be on the beach. She'd been too embarrassed to ask.

At six-thirty sharp, the "Reel Southern Ladies" headed off.

The rain had stopped, and the clouds were breaking up just enough to allow the first bit of daylight to come through. But the wind had not stopped.

"Will it be this windy all day?" Jenni asked timidly.

"It might back off a little," replied May Ellen, looking at her phone. "Hmm…Weather Channel says ten to fifteen from the northeast all day. That's not terrible, but out there on the beach, you'll feel it, especially if it's more on the fifteen side of things."

Jenni tried, and failed, to figure out a way to capture the warmth of the truck and keep it with her. She felt herself begin to pout as they turned back into the campground, following the road down the ramp onto the beach where she and Caitlin had practiced yesterday.

Barb told them at dinner last night that they would be on the south side for the morning and the north side for the afternoon. On Saturday morning, they would be back on the north side but not as far away.

Jenni wondered how Barb would know exactly where to park, but she soon found out.

There was a stream of four-by-fours heading over the ramp. There were markers with numbers, in order, on the sand.

"See those," pointed Caitlin. "It's like I mentioned to you yesterday, but you probably don't remember, with everything that I put into your head. We are number 112, so we'll look for that number, and we can fish in between the stakes with our number. The teams next to us will be 111 and 113.

Jenni nodded and watched as the four-wheel drives turned off into their slots. The numbers had started at 120, so she knew they wouldn't have too far to go.

Sure enough, Barb eased the truck into slot 112 and announced it was time to unpack and set up. She had made it clear there could be no fishing before seven, that was strictly forbidden, but they could get everything ready.

Jenni's bathroom question was immediately answered when Barb and May Ellen put up the strangest tent she'd ever seen. "Is that what I think it is?"

Caitlin laughed. "If you're thinking 'bathroom', you're right." Caitlin elbowed Jenni. "And aren't you glad?"

Jenni nodded and was as thankful as she'd ever been for a piece of outdoor equipment. They had parked in the center of their allotted area, so she assumed two of them would fish on one side and two on the other. She glanced over and noticed a group of men and women, a mixed team, setting up at 111. As far as she could tell, no one was in 113, so maybe they wouldn't show up, and she could fish at that end.

As Barb and May Ellen seemed to have things under control, she grabbed Caitlin's arm and pointed to where she'd hoped to be. "How 'bout I fish on this side?"

"Whatever you want," said Caitlin. "Let's walk over

there and see what you'll be casting into. If there's a bit of a hole there, you'll be in luck."

They wandered over to the stakes between 112 and 113 and looked out. The wind was incessant, and Jenni was so thankful they had outfitted her appropriately.

She was cold enough with the layers she had on. Without that flannel shirt and her hat, she'd be frozen.

Caitlin slipped her arm through Jenni's and looked at her friend. "It's beautiful out here in its own way. Try to just enjoy the day. The three of us, I mean Aunt May Ellen, Mom, and me, we'll hopefully catch plenty. And if you do, that's great. If you don't, that's OK too. You made it possible for us to be here, and we're grateful. Especially those two." She pointed to Barb and May Ellen whose heads were deep into their tackle boxes.

Jenni was just about to respond when a truck pulled into space 113, spraying sand everywhere. Four guys tumbled out, laughing and yelling and basically making themselves known. One of them loudly announced to no one in particular, "Get ready everyone. The "Cast of Thousands" is here. Tournament is over."

Jenni looked sadly at the truck, realizing her dream of fishing in isolation had quickly been shattered.

Then she did a double-take. It was *that* truck, that Ford F-150. She knew that truck. Under her breath, she muttered, "I can't believe it."

"What?" asked Caitlin.

But before Jenni could answer and make a get-away, one of the four walked over with a bright smile and said, "Good morning, ladies. I always like to introduce myself to the neighbors for the morning session. I... Oh." He stopped, then grinning broadly, continued, "Well, if it isn't the last person on earth?"

Chapter Six

No. No. No! This can't be happening!

Despite the chill, Jenni's cheeks burned making them probably as pink as her hat.

"It's Jenni, isn't it?" the man said. "I know you remember me."

Jenni looked at Caleb and then at Caitlin and gave a sheepish grin. "Yes, I'm Jenni, and this is my friend Caitlin. And yes, I told you I'd be the last person on earth you'd see at a fishing tournament, but plans changed. And here I am."

In his fishing waders and goofy woolen hat, he was even more gorgeous than she remembered. She struggled to keep from just staring at him. Her mouth remained open, but no more words would come out.

Thankfully, Caleb seemed not to notice Jenni's reaction. He reached out and shook Caitlin's hand.

Caitlin had been watching this exchange with some confusion. Then the penny dropped. "You are the guy who helped Jenni out of the sand!"

"Oh, she told you about that, did she?" He laughed.

Jenni was stuck wondering how anyone could look so good in fishing attire while she, in her humble opinion, looked like a clown. "We thought she might keep that a deep, dark secret."

"Nope, one thing about Jen is that she is very honest," said Caitlin, grabbing her friend's arm. "Just one of the many things she's known for."

"Is that a fact?" replied Caleb. He seemed to want to say something further, but the rest of his teammates were yelling for him to return.

"I guess I'd better go." He half-turned. "But just for the record, those idiots are my college buddies Johan, Bertrand—we call him Bertie—and Lyle. They are loud, but they are harmless. I'd love to hear your story sometime, Jenni, about how you ended up out here. For a first-time angler, which is what I have to assume you are, you're pretty brave. Good luck."

Jenni blushed. "Caitlin was good enough to give me lessons yesterday. We'll see. Um, good luck to you too."

Jenni sincerely hoped that with the wind and the pounding surf, Caleb was out of earshot when Caitlin nearly squealed, "He's gorgeous, Jenni. Just how did you omit that from your story Wednesday night?"

"Is he?" Jenni asked. She was unwilling to let her own feelings be known, whatever they were. She had already placed Caleb in the recesses of her mind. Or she thought she had.

Knowing he was right next to her for the next several hours might make things challenging, but she could focus on fishing, and she'd be fine. "I mean, I guess so. I really wasn't paying that much attention, you know, with being stuck and all."

Jenni adjusted one of the straps on her waders.

No use in admitting the truth. After all, what would that mean? Better to just move on.

"Jenni, I just refuse to believe you have shut out that much of your life. You have to allow yourself to feel again," Caitlin said sternly. Then her tone grew softer. "Hey, I think it's almost seven, and Mom and May Ellen will want to give us the team spirit talk. Breathe, Jenni. It's OK. I just wish I'd claimed this spot to fish. Lots of eye candy over there." She winked.

They walked back to the truck, and Caitlin told her mother and aunt about their angler buddies in the next slot.

"What a nice coincidence," Barb said. "But now we're ready for action. Let's catch some fish!"

Jenni grabbed her rod and her bait and made her way to her designated spot. She tried not to look to her right, but she couldn't help but notice that Caleb had picked the spot in his slot furthest to the left, maybe so he could see her clearly?

She took a deep breath, dug her gloves out of her pockets, and began to bait her hook. It wasn't easy, but she finally got a piece which she felt would stay on.

This isn't rocket science.

She made her way down to the water's edge.

She watched as her three teammates stepped onto the surf and cast out. They made it look so easy.

She moved the rod back and with all her strength, she cast out. She saw the sinker and bait head way out over the breakers, and for a split second, she was elated. She had made a great cast.

But then something felt terribly wrong. She looked up at the rod tip and saw her line dangling there forlornly. With a sinking feeling, she realized what she had, or actually hadn't done. She hadn't flipped the bail.

She was mortified, especially when she heard a voice call out, "You need to flip the bail, Jenni. Fishing 101."

It was Caleb. Of course, it was. She heard his buddies laughing. She wanted to crawl into the sand like a crab, but she squared her shoulders and walked back to the truck.

She and Caitlin had prepared several rigs and now she had to remember how to replace what she'd lost. Caitlin walked up behind her and shook her head.

"I'm not surprised you did that," Caitlin said. "We all do it at one time or another. "

"I'm just so stupid," Jenni responded bitterly. "I knew I'd mess up. Compy always said..."

"Enough," snapped Caitlin. "Just listen to how I tell you to make the knots and let's get you back out there fishing."

Jenni's fingers were cold, but she managed, only because Caitlin was not only the most patient instructor, but she knew exactly what to say so that Jenni understood.

As she walked back over to her spot, she glanced over at Caleb. One of his teammates had already caught a fish, and there was the requisite back-slapping and carrying-on.

Good, he's occupied. I will take my time and I will remember what Caitlin told me and I will not worry about Caleb watching me or not watching me because it doesn't matter.

This time, she was very careful to flip the bail, and her cast, while not spectacular, got into the water.

"That's better," she heard Caleb call out. "I do that at least once a tournament myself."

Jenni wanted to respond but then decided not to. She just nodded. She wanted to be in her own fishing bubble. That's where she'd stay.

Chapter Seven

From time to time, she'd hear shouts from the different teams as fish were caught and measured, and when Barb caught the first fish, a nice puppy drum, Jenni cheered loudly and gave her a big hug.

They had about thirty minutes to go when Jenni cast out and suddenly felt an incessant, hard tug in her line. "Hey, hey, hey!" she hollered to Caitlin, "I think I have caught something. Now what?"

Caitlin placed her rod in its holder and ran over. "You have something on for sure. Start reeling it in. Keep your tip up and keep reeling."

Jenni couldn't believe the excitement she felt.

She thought she could hear Caleb cheering her on, but she couldn't be certain. She had to focus. She wouldn't mess this up. She kept reeling and reeling and didn't seem to be making much progress, but eventually, she could see something thrashing in the water.

"Bring it all the way in," Caitlin commanded. "You have to bring it in and get it off the hook yourself."

When she finally brought it up on the beach, Jenni was appalled. She'd never seen anything quite like what was on her hook. And when she grabbed it, it swelled up like a balloon. "What is this?" she screamed at Caitlin.

Caitlin, Mary Ellen, and Barb were, she realized, doubled over with laughter.

"It's a blow toad," said Caitlin. "Or a puffer fish. It's trash, so just try to remove the hook as gently as you can and throw it back in."

Jenni struggled with the hook, but finally, it came free, and she walked the little monster to the edge of the surf where he swam away.

At least I didn't kill it.

As she walked back to her rod, she noticed Caleb walking over.

"Well now, this session is just about done, and you caught yourself a blow toad. Ugly little devils, aren't they? You know, catching something, anything, is a pretty neat feeling. I assume that would be your first fish?"

"Yes," said Jenni coolly, realizing that yes, he'd watched the entire escapade with her fish. "I'm sure y'all have caught plenty of real fish this morning."

"It's been pretty good," admitted Caleb, scanning the water. "But I've seen your team pull in a few as well. We'll be up just south of Salvo for the afternoon. What about you?"

"Avon," Jenni said, breathing a sigh of relief. She could fish without him being a distraction.

"Well, have a good afternoon, and keep having fun. You're okay, Jenni. Gotta hand it to you."

Jenni said nothing as he walked away. She took out her phone and noticed it was almost eleven-thirty. Without casting again, she walked over to the truck and began to get ready for the drive up to Avon.

He's just too nice. What am I missing? She asked herself. *And why do I care?*

I really made a fool of myself again. A blow toad. Of all the creatures in the sea.

Caitlin walked over and put her arm around Jenni. "You've had quite a morning. I am pretty proud of you," she said. "And I think there's a certain fisherman who would like to catch you."

Jenni just shook her head and helped everyone pack up. As they were ready to leave, Caleb's truck passed in front of them, and he beeped his horn and waved. Caitlin waved back enthusiastically, but Jenni only held up her hand in acknowledgment.

By Friday night, Jenni was so cold and tired that she went to bed directly after dinner. The team had done well, but not well enough to be in the top five. She hadn't caught any more fish, but she hadn't lost any more rigs either. She was finally getting used to baiting the hook, and her casting seemed to be getting smoother.

Friday afternoon their neighbors had been another team of women and they enjoyed bantering back and forth. Barb had said they'd leave at the same time Saturday morning, so she was only too ready to take a hot shower and try to get some sleep.

She had dreams of puffer fish and trophies and Compy and Caleb fighting over a fishing rod. When her phone alarm went off at five-thirty, she felt as though she hadn't slept at all.

The weather was still a bit brisk but there was more sun than on Friday, and she was extremely happy about that. Their Saturday spot was near Ramp 44, which many considered a prime spot.

The tournament organizers tried to be sure people got moved around a good bit even though it was considered to be one of the shorter tournaments. But Ramp 44 was near the famous Point, and she was hopeful the team could make some progress up the leaderboard.

When they pulled into their slot, she thought she recognized Chris and Susan Smith as their judges for the day. Sure enough, when they saw Barb's truck, they stopped by to exchange hellos and ask about how the team had done.

"Well, Jenni caught a blow toad," Barb reported. Jenni cringed.

"What a great way to start," laughed Chris. "Just holler for us when you catch that big one."

Jenni smiled, and the ladies began to set up their area.

Jenni noted with satisfaction that Caleb and his merry men were nowhere to be found. The sun was coming out from behind the clouds and, all in all, Jenni had to admit she was enjoying herself. She caught one or two mullets that were just long enough to measure, and she felt a growing sense of pride that she was contributing. By the end of the session, they all felt confident they had a successful morning.

"How do we find out how we did?" Jenni asked as they

headed home. She was blissfully happy that this was the end of her fishing, and that she could now enjoy the afternoon with a good book and a glass of wine.

"At the banquet," the others all said in unison.

"It's a good time," said Barb, pulling into the driveway. "You'll want to rest up this afternoon. It starts at six-thirty. There's a fantastic buffet, and they draw for door prizes too."

Jenni started to say that she really had no intention of going to the banquet, that she'd had quite enough of fishing. But she knew that her team expected her to go, and she couldn't let them down now. She could still get some rest before they had to leave.

Chapter Eight

The banquet, thankfully, was not a dress-up affair.

As she dressed for it, Jenni struggled with her emotions.

Would she see Caleb there? Did she want to see him there? Even with all of the catastrophes that seemed to surround her interactions with him, he didn't make her feel useless or stupid like Compy always had.

He laughed with her, and not at her. That was a big difference. It made her feel a bit more like her old self, more carefree and more willing to just roll with the punches.

She had missed that about herself.

Here was a guy she barely knew, and he was making her feel good about herself again, even if it was just a little bit.

When they all walked out the door at six-fifteen to go to the community center, Jenni actually did feel rested and perhaps even happy. She had a sense of accomplishment that she hadn't felt in a long time.

The hall was packed when they walked inside, and Jenni finally grasped the number of people who had been in the tournament.

The noise from conversations was deafening, so as they waited at their table to get into the buffet line, she scanned the room and enjoyed the people-watching.

She caught sight of Chris and Susan Smith and SeaAnna and Mike Leonard at their table, and she assumed the young couple with them was Dare Davis and JoBell Leonard. They seemed to be deeply engaged in conversation with each other. There was a level of comfort there, Jenni felt, that reflected a relationship that was filled with caring and mutual respect. She could just sense it.

It wasn't until she was in the buffet line that she spotted Caleb and the rest of the "Cast of Thousands."

They were tucked away at a table in a corner near one of the exits and were talking with the anglers at nearby tables.

He looked up and waved and started making his way toward her.

It was so crowded that all the tables were practically touching, making walking very tricky.

"I don't want to hold you up." He smiled. "But I just wanted to say that I really was impressed with your efforts today. It takes a lot of nerve to fish for the first time in your life in a tournament."

Jenni blushed. "Thanks for that. It was an interesting

day for sure. I guess I learned a lot. I won't be making that bail mistake any time soon."

"Don't be hard on yourself if it happens again. Like I said, I've done it before, and I'll do it again. You get all excited in the moment and, well, sometimes you forget. Just take it in stride."

He began moving away. "I don't want to hold up the food line. But remember, you really did alright."

Jenni's heart was beating hard, and she once again was at a loss for words.

I did alright.

She almost felt giddy.

She carefully placed the food on her plate, trying to balance everything just so. Buffet lines were never her forte.

She was making her way back to the table when Caleb waved to her again as he was sitting down next to his friends.

She smiled at him and missed it when another person, already seated, pushed their chair back, causing her not only to trip but to send her food flying in several directions.

The ensuing chaos lasted only a few minutes, but for Jenni, everything seemed in slow motion. There were assurances that everyone was OK, a new plate of food was delivered to her, and the food, which thankfully landed on the floor and not on someone, was quickly cleaned up.

Jenni was disconsolate. She had done just what Compy would have expected her to do. She made a fool of herself once more.

She spent the rest of the evening barely speaking to Caitlin, Barb, or May Ellen.

Her mood did not improve when she learned that they did not make the top five.

While the rest of the team seemed to take it in stride

and seemed extremely happy with their seventh-place finish, Jenni could only focus on the fact that, once again, she had been the center of attention but for the wrong reason.

When the event neared its end, she asked Barb for the truck keys and began to make her way to the exit.

Caleb jumped up from his seat and tried to intercept her, but she ignored him and ran as quickly as she could to the truck.

She briefly glanced behind her, but he had stopped at the doorway and just seemed to shrug.

Jenni was too ashamed to walk back to speak to him. When Caitlin and the others rejoined her, not even May Ellen winning a new rod as a door prize lifted her spirits.

They seemed to know she needed her space and didn't push when she said little on the ride back to the "Mermaid's Mansion."

Jenni excused herself politely when they got home and went straight to bed.

In the morning, she apologized at breakfast for causing such a scene and despite their assurances that she did no such thing, Jenni decided not to spend the morning there but just to head back to Raleigh. She thanked Barb profusely, hugged her and May Ellen, and then headed to her car.

Caitlin followed her and stood by her door.

Jenni put down the window and knew what was coming.

"Jenni, I can't make you happy," Caitlin began. "No one can. Only you can do that. But you let everything get to you, and then you act like it's always your fault. I've never seen you with such low self-confidence and self-esteem. It's just not you."

Caitlin reached into the car and patted her friend on the shoulder. "I had hoped this weekend would be a breath of fresh air, no pun intended. A new start. We had a lot of fun. Please think about what I've said. You have so much going for you."

"Thanks, CayCay." A tear ran down Jenni's face. "It was, as you said, a weekend I'll never forget. And maybe in time, I'll only remember the fun parts. I'll try. And I'll keep in touch. Give my best to Andrew, and your dad too. I'm sure he was glad to be at home and away from this crazy crew."

She waved as she pulled out of the driveway, and then headed north on Highway 12.

She couldn't wait to get back to her own place, to try to put things into perspective, and to get back to work.

She could get lost there and leave the memories of bait, bails, puffer fish, and a certain fisherman, far behind.

Chapter Nine

Jenni was once again confused when she woke up.

Was it time to get ready to go out on the beach?

As she opened one eye and looked out her apartment window, she remembered she was back home in Raleigh and today was Monday. Monday meant work.

She quickly checked her phone to be sure she hadn't overslept, but actually, she was ahead of the alarm. The last few days of getting up so early had stayed with her. But rather than go back to sleep, she'd use the extra time to take a long shower and reflect on the last few days.

On the drive back from the Outer Banks to Raleigh,

which had been mercifully uneventful, she reflected on what had happened to her and her reactions to everything. She also gave credence to Caitlin's admonitions to her because Caitlin was her dear friend.

Jenni knew she had Jenni's best interests at heart. But Caitlin also had never had her heart broken as Jenni had, so she really couldn't put herself totally in Jenni's shoes.

How long does it take to get over a failed marriage? How long does it take to trust again?

When would she start dismantling the walls she had so carefully built around herself over the last year?

And what about Caleb?

There had been not one negative in her time with him if she was going to be honest with herself.

He wasn't at all like Compy, though she continually tried to put him in that mold.

But she couldn't let herself go down that road of hoping or caring or desiring ever again. Clearly, she wasn't made for a relationship.

She stepped out of the shower and towel-dried her hair.

But why, then, was she still thinking about him? Maybe it was because this past weekend had turned out to be so unexpected. He was just part of all the craziness.

Yes, that was probably it. Today it was back to work at *Raleigh Wins,* and that would consume all of her thoughts.

Raleigh Wins was an amazing non-profit getting ready to celebrate its fiftieth year. It was a youth-centered organization that she totally believed made a difference in the lives of teens in the Raleigh-Durham-Chapel Hill Triangle area.

She'd met the kids and read the testimonials. She saw the results.

She felt extremely lucky to have landed the position of

development director, which opened up as she was moving back from Columbia. The former development director was retiring, and they were looking for a replacement. Jenni had interned and volunteered at many non-profits from the time she was at St. Adrian's, and had garnered enough experience to get hired.

She loved her boss, Dee, the CEO.

Jenni was happy that she spent most of her days in the office or working from home with donor lists and campaign charts and spreadsheets.

Dee was the face of the organization and made many of the donor calls herself. For now, that suited Jenni.

She didn't have the confidence to meet potential donors face-to-face. The old Jenni would have, and she hoped that in time, she'd regain some of her old self again.

She finished her coffee and headed to her office downtown. She hadn't planned on going into the office that morning—*Are my hands still smelling like fish? No, that has to be my imagination*—but an early morning email from Dee requesting her presence had changed that.

Walking into the hallway that housed her office, she was surprised to see Dee waiting for her.

She knew she wasn't late, so this had to be something very important.

Jenni wracked her brain and came up blank. It must have shown on her face because Dee said, "Jenni, you look terrified. I just need a favor."

"Sure, Dee, what's up?" She looked carefully at her boss. Dee had dark circles under her eyes, and she looked like she had slept in her clothes. She also looked like she had been crying.

"It's my mom," said Dee slowly. "I was with her all this weekend at her care home. She's just not doing well. I thought I could catch up on a few things this morning, but Gentle River just called me, and they've taken her to the hospital again. I have to go."

Jenni nodded. Dee's mother had been struggling with Alzheimer's for years, and it had been a steady decline. Her dad was long out of the picture, having divorced Dee's mom when Dee was younger, and her siblings were all out of state. It fell to Dee to handle it all, as far as Jenni could tell.

"I need you to handle an appointment for me," Dee was saying. "It has taken me forever to set this up, and I can't simply cancel. Second Bank has never really been a supporter of ours, but they have a new CEO who actually agreed to meet me about doing something for the fiftieth-anniversary gala. I am not expecting much, but any donation would get our foot in the door for the future. I need you to go and make the pitch."

Jenni started to open her mouth, but Dee continued.

"I know you weren't expecting this, but I left some information about the bank on your desk. The appointment is at ten-thirty, so you'll have time to review everything about their corporate giving, their likes and dislikes in terms of mission, and that sort of thing. You have all the gala information and our pitch piece. I am not sure if I can be back today or not, but you can brief me in the morning. I hope I'll be back in tomorrow."

"OK," said Jenni without much conviction. "Of course, I'll do it."

Dee looked at her and said carefully, "Jenni, it's time you started getting out. Development work is people work. You do a great job behind the scenes, but you need to be on the scene. I just can't do it all. The organization is growing, and our gala is a huge deal. The board is expecting big things based on our previous successes. I know that you can handle this."

Jenni reached out and hugged Dee. "I will do my level best. You need to take care of yourself and your mom. Don't worry about me. But before you go, who is the CEO?"

"William, or I guess, Bill Ragland," Dee responded. "But Mr. Ragland for you." Then she fished in her pocket for her car keys and looked at Jenni expectantly.

"Got it. Mr. Ragland," Jenni confirmed. "Now go."

She walked into her office and saw the paperwork Dee had left for her on her desk.

It was nine-fifteen now, so she had about an hour to do some research. She wished she had dressed a little more appropriately for a call, but at least she wasn't in waders and a flannel shirt.

She delved into the materials and tried to absorb the pertinent details. She shook her head and laughed to herself. It was another crash course.

Chapter Ten

The corporate offices of Second Bank were within walking distance. It was a bright spring morning, and Jenni tried to use the beauty of the day as positive motivation for what she was going to do.

When she got to the address, she realized it was a high rise, so she had to check the listing on the wall by the elevators to find the correct floor.

Stepping out on the tenth floor, she walked into a well-appointed seating area with a very well-dressed receptionist.

She looked up at Jenni and inquired, "What can I do for you?"

Jenni smiled and tried to look as professional as possible. "I'm Jenni Kirk from Raleigh Wins. I'm here on behalf of Dee Carroll who unfortunately had a family emergency this morning. I'm here to see Mr. Ragland."

The receptionist shook her head. "I'm sorry, but Mr. Ragland called in sick this morning."

Then she brightened. "But he did make arrangements for you to meet with our VP of Corporate Relations, Mr. Prescott. I'll buzz him to let him know you're here. Go through these doors, and his office will be in the suite at the end of the hall on your right."

Jenni waited until she heard the security lock click before opening the door and proceeding down the hallway.

The offices were all glassed in, glass doors to enter, and clearly lots of glass windows opposite to see the Raleigh skyline.

She got to the suite at the end of the hall and noted she had to pull the door to enter, which she promptly pushed, meaning she walked into a solid panel of glass. Shaking her head, and hoping no one had noticed, she tried again and stepped inside the office finding herself face-to-face with one Caleb Prescott.

She was shocked.

In her mind, she knew she had wanted to see him again. She felt such a strong attraction. But he made her crazy at the same time. She did ridiculous things when she was around him. And there was that chance of hurt. That chance she was unwilling to take.

They both stared at each other for what felt like an eternity, although it was really just a few seconds before Caleb recovered and chuckled. "Well, well. Now I know your last name too, Ms. Jenni Kirk. I have to say, this is really a coincidence. Those pull-instead-of-push instructions can be confusing. Please, have a seat. Water?"

Jenni declined, and Caleb nodded.

He's probably glad I didn't take any because with my history I'd spill it, she thought. *And how can he look so put together after a weekend of hellraising and fishing with his friends?*

As if he was reading her mind, Caleb said, "I left Hatteras right after the banquet on Saturday. I wanted to have a full day to recover from the weekend's festivities. It was tiring making the drive, but it sure felt good to have yesterday to recover."

Jenni noted the wisdom in that. "I, uh, got home yesterday but I guess the fishing got the best of me. I am still tired."

Caleb laughed. "I'm sorry if I caused your calamity Saturday. I shouldn't have distracted you. Navigating that room was an obstacle course."

"Oh, you didn't distract me," she said, making sure he got the message. "I guess I am just terminally clumsy." But she could feel the heat creeping up her neck. She did not want him to think he had the power to distract her.

"I ran after you, you know. I wanted to tell you that I enjoyed meeting you.

"Well, I'd had enough, I'm afraid.

"You should have hung around. And your team did really well, seventh place ain't too shabby," he said with a bit of a country twang. "I'm proud of you! I'm not even sure where we ended up, but it was a great time."

"My friend and her family are very good anglers," Jenni said, shifting in her chair. "I was just the tag-along." She needed to get this conversation back on track. "I'm sure you've got other appointments today, especially with Mr. Ragland's illness, so I won't take up much of your time."

Caleb leaned back in his chair and smiled. "You take all the time you need, Jenni Kirk. Now, tell me why you're here."

On firmer footing, Jenni launched into her presentation. Because she loved what she did and believed so firmly in the cause, she spoke passionately but convincingly. She ended by expressing what Dee had said to her earlier in the day but adding a bit from the research she'd done just an hour or so prior.

"This gala, this anniversary, means a tremendous amount to us. The founder of the organization will be there. She's not in the best of health, so we want this to be a positive event for her. But we also want to use it as a springboard for our major capital campaign next year. I know that Second Bank hasn't supported us in the past, but we have a number of giving levels from which to choose. I'm hopeful you can discuss this with Mr. Ragland and find a level that's comfortable for the bank. I have also noted that teens play a role in your mission for community needs fulfillment, so this seems like a good fit."

Caleb said nothing, and Jenni wondered if she had overstepped her bounds or had somehow said something inappropriate. Finally, he pushed his chair back and placed his hands on the desk.

"That was quite a spiel," he began.

Jenni was not happy with the choice of "spiel," but she didn't interrupt. "Our charitable giving budget is pretty much set, but I think we have some leeway for discretionary giving," he went on. "That's under Mr. Ragland's control. I'll certainly pass this along. Thanks for your time."

Jenni was pretty sure she was being dismissed. She

collected herself and began to stand up, frantically trying to remember whether she should push or pull on the door going out. But Caleb wasn't finished. He shifted his weight and cocked his head to one side. The sun shining in the window framed him almost in a glow, and once again Jenni realized how handsome he was.

"And so, Ms. Kirk, we are done with the business part of this meeting," he said. "But onto something less intense and much more pleasurable, would you care to join me for a drink tomorrow night after work?"

She desperately wanted to say yes, but she just couldn't risk it. "I'm sorry, I can't. I have a class to teach."

She realized that her tone had been abrupt, too abrupt.

Caleb picked up on that immediately.

"Sure, that's fine," he said. "Maybe another time?"

Jenni only nodded in a manner that could have been a yes or a no. "Thank you again for your time, Caleb. We'll be grateful for your consideration."

They shook hands awkwardly, and she began to walk toward the door, but Caleb moved around his desk and got there before she did. "Going out, it's push," he said, as he opened the door for her and smiled. "It's been great to see you again."

Her shoulder brushed his as she passed through the door, and she felt the smallest jolt of electricity.

She mumbled, "Thanks," and didn't turn around as she walked back into the reception area.

She wanted to seem aloof and in control even if inside she didn't feel that way at all.

If she had looked back, she would have seen Caleb still watching her, all the way down the hall.

Chapter Eleven

It was Wednesday morning when, once again, her boss was waiting for Jenni when she arrived at her office. This time, Dee looked a little more well-rested and seemed to be in a more positive frame of mind.

"Good morning, Jenni," she said. "I'd like to talk to you in my office, so grab a cup of coffee and come on by."

Jenni was glad for the chance to have that second cup, but she was uncertain as to what this early morning conference could mean. More than likely, Dee would want an update on sponsorships.

As she hadn't heard anything back from Second Bank,

she assumed her efforts had not amounted to much. She wondered if Caleb had even talked to Mr. Ragland about her presentation.

Dee was sitting behind her desk, and Jenni had barely sat down across from her when she said, "I have no idea what you said to the gentleman you met with Monday morning, but you must have made one hell of an impression."

Jenni said nothing, still not sure whether making an impression was related to almost walking through a glass door, or whether the bank would actually be donating something for the gala.

"I had a call from Bill Ragland yesterday right after five," Dee was saying. "I almost didn't pick up the phone, but I am sure glad I did. Apparently, he had just met with one Caleb Prescott who recommended not just that they contribute to the gala, but to be a presenting sponsor."

She stopped and let the words sink in.

Jenni was speechless. She felt her heart skip a beat and her mind started to play out scenarios of what Caleb may have said about her.

Realizing she wasn't really paying attention to Dee, she reigned in her thoughts and sat even more upright.

Dee went on. "He said that Prescott was genuinely impressed with your presentation and felt it would be in the bank's best interests to take on a very high level of sponsorship. This is just incredible. I'm so happy, but I am also so proud of you. I knew you needed to start getting out!"

Jenni didn't know what to say. She knew she should be thrilled. Obtaining a presenting sponsorship was quite a coup, especially since their long-time major sponsor had pulled the plug a few weeks ago due to an economic downturn in their business.

Dee had been frantic, and these past few weeks she had been focused on trying to find a replacement. Now one had dropped into their laps quite unexpectedly.

But this also might mean she would be dealing with Caleb regularly in the run-up to the event. She wasn't sure how she felt about that at all.

"I told Ragland you'd be in touch soon to begin to work out the details of how they would like their sponsorship to look. I will work with you, but I know you'll have ideas as well, and you'll be the point person. We'll want to keep them informed every step of the way and make sure that they feel this sponsorship is as beneficial to the bank as it is for us. I suggest you get some thoughts together, and then give Caleb Prescott a call. You can go from there."

She stood up and walked around her desk and gave Jenni a warm hug. "You know I've had so much on my mind with my mom that I haven't been able to think about the gala as much as I should have. This is a big deal for us, and it takes so much off my plate. Thank you so much, Jenni."

Jenni walked back to her office, shut the door, and for several minutes just stared at nothing at all.

Was Caleb's support a way to test her? To see her fail? Why would he do that? He barely knew her.

She was being ridiculous.

None of that mattered now anyway. Her role was to get the gala together and see that it was a big success, and if that meant working with him, so be it.

She opened up her laptop and began listing all of the things that would need to be done, and some questions she would need answered right away before she could proceed.

Normally, this challenge would have meant Jenni was laser-focused on the task in front of her, but she found her thoughts drifting.

Obviously, she'd paid more attention to Caleb Prescott than she'd admitted.

Caleb had that sweet, slightly crooked smile that she found attractive to the point of being almost seductive. She had noted his eyes were hazel and that they crinkled up at the corners when he laughed, which she realized was quite often.

Seeing him in a suit only emphasized how in-shape he was, and how did he have a tan already? It was just April.

She could almost feel her fingers running through that sandy hair.

Stop it, she said to herself. *You are a professional, and you are way out of line here. This is business, and important business at that.*

She went to the office kitchen for a bottle of water, took a gulp, and then took a few deep breaths.

"Are you alright?" Dee asked. She was so lost in thought that she didn't even realize someone else was in the room. "Your face is so red! Do you have a fever?"

"I'm fine," Jenni stammered. "You know me. I've been really doing some intense planning, and I guess I must have gotten into it more than I realized. But I want to be ready for my call."

"Oh, right," said Dee. "Well, don't get that wound up. You look like you're ready to pass out. I'll need you at one hundred percent from now until the gala."

"Absolutely," nodded Jenni. "Off I go. I'll let you know how it goes." And with that, she took the water bottle with her and headed back to her office.

She looked at her phone for several moments and then called the bank. The voice at the other end of the line no doubt belonged to the classy receptionist she had met on Monday.

Jenni explained who she was and the reason for her call. She felt her stomach lurch as she was transferred to Caleb's office.

"Caleb Prescott's office," the voice answered.

"Hi this is Jenni Kirk with Raleigh Wins," she began. "I'm calling for Mr. Prescott."

"Oh, Miss Kirk. Hi, this is Tory Lee, Mr. Prescott's assistant," said the voice that now had a name. "He told me you'd probably be calling. I'm sorry, but he's out of town for the rest of the week at a conference in Atlanta. But he told me to let you know you'd be working with me on our gala sponsorship. Feel free to call me Tory."

"Ah, well, that's...that's great," Jenni stuttered. "I mean, that's fine. Of course."

"Well," said Tory. "Between his traveling and his teaching, you were really lucky to catch him on Monday. But you know how it is, I really do all the work anyway." Tory laughed.

Jenni was having trouble sorting through her emotions. She wasn't sure if she was immensely relieved or disappointed.

She convinced herself she was definitely relieved. She had no reason to want to be involved with Caleb Prescott any more than she had to be.

She and Tory chatted for a few more moments. Tory agreed to come to Jenni's office on Friday and they'd spend the afternoon working on details. That would give them both time to think.

Jenni ended the call with a "Thank you" and put her head on her desk.

Of course, she'd be working with his assistant. What had she been thinking? As the Vice President of Corporate

Relations, he had more important things to tend to. And teaching a class? What was that all about?

She pulled up Google on her computer and typed in his name.

There were several hits, and it didn't take Jenni long to realize Caleb Prescott was on the fast track at Second Bank, and that he was definitely an up-and-comer in Raleigh. A quick scan of his bio showed graduation from a fine prep school, undergrad at the University of North Carolina at Chapel Hill, and an MBA from the Darden School at the University of Virginia. He definitely had credentials.

He'd been named as one of the "Forty Under Forty" making a difference in Raleigh, and she noted that based on the various dates mentioned, they were about the same age. She found no mention of any spouse, past or current, which jived with the fact that she'd been sure to check back in Hatteras if he wore a ring.

She also saw that indeed he taught some undergrad classes in basic business at community colleges in the area.

Jenni clicked out of the search engine and closed the lid of her computer.

Chapter Twelve

He was absolutely out of her league, no doubt about that. Her teaching a class was in no way comparable to what he did.

She thought for a brief moment about Compy, and how he'd convinced her not to go on to grad school. She felt as though she had wasted so many years playing socialite in South Carolina. But then, she'd made that choice. She probably could have insisted on going to school, but at first, she enjoyed the life she had with Compy. It was nice being the wife of an attorney and basking in all the perks that came with that lifestyle.

But it also meant that she lost those years. She wondered if she'd ever regain what she felt she'd lost.

There was not much sense in dwelling on that now.

The gala was about six weeks away, at the end of May. Between now and then, she and Tory would be spending a lot of time together but thankfully, after this initial meeting, nearly everything could be done by email.

It certainly wouldn't come from Jenni that she and "Mr. Prescott" had met in the not-so-distant past. It would be better to keep that under wraps from the staff at Second Southern, and Dee too.

Deep down, she was disappointed at not working with him directly, but it would never show.

Tory turned out to be a very bright and witty young woman with plenty of ideas about how the bank wanted the sponsorship to look. She challenged many of Jenni's ideas.

At first, Jenni wasn't sure they'd work well together but by the end of their first meeting at Jenni's office, she felt the relationship would work out just fine. She was impressed that someone who was obviously younger than her had the self-confidence to hold her own. Tory also had a great sense of humor which would be helpful, Jenni knew, when they got down to crunch time.

They were finishing up their conversation when Tory looked at Jenni and said, "Mr. Prescott said he met you recently on the Outer Banks."

Jenni felt her face redden. "Oh, it was really just a few chance meetings," she said dismissively.

"Huh," said Tory, looking doubtful. "I've been working with Mr. Prescott for a few years now, so not terribly long, but long enough to know that when he mentions something personal like that, I take note."

Jenni looked at Tory and smiled. "Well, I'm sure Mr.

Prescott meets a lot of people given his position and how busy he must be. But this was just a fishing tournament that I unexpectedly found myself involved in. It was really just sort of a passing thing."

For one brief moment, she allowed herself to be flattered that he'd mentioned her.

Maybe he *was* interested in her in a good way.

But no, he was a businessman who probably—no, absolutely—met a ton of people. All potential clients. Not potential partners.

Tory gathered her belongings and looked at Jenni with a trace of a smile on her face. "I see," she said. "Well, it's been a good meeting today and nice meeting you, Jenni. I'll get back to you next week and let you know which one of these ideas we'll run with."

Jenni watched her leave and then began collecting her sweater, laptop bag, and purse, as well as her thoughts.

She was very thankful the meeting had lasted right up until five. Now it was the weekend, and she could relax a bit. But what was she going to do?

That evening she tried to get into the latest binge-worthy show on Netflix, but her thoughts kept returning to Hatteras. She had received a text from Caitlin asking how the week back at work had gone, and if she had recovered from the tournament.

Jenni hesitated and then picked up the phone. In her opinion, sometimes a call was so much better than a text.

"Hey CayCay," she said dwhen Caitlin answered. "It's your ol' fishin' buddy."

Caitlin laughed. "Yes, I know it's you. To what do I owe this honor? It's Friday night. Why aren't you out kicking your heels celebrating the fact that you don't have to fish in the morning?"

"I'm celebrating all right, but it's just me and the TV and a nice glass of pinot noir," said Jenni. She moved a pillow behind her back and stretched her legs out on her couch. "I had what you might say was a very interesting week, and I just had to share."

"Do tell," said Caitlin.

Jenni thought she heard Andrew in the background, and this was confirmed when Caitlin asked for a refill. "Andrew is waiting on me tonight. My adult beverage of choice is Chardonnay. I have a feeling I might need at least one more while you share."

"You might," said Jenni, and she relayed to Caitlin the events of the week beginning with

the surprise meeting with Caleb at the bank, to the news of the sponsorship, to the meeting with Tory that afternoon.

Caitlin gasped, laughed, and murmured various "oh nos" and "no ways" as Jenni spoke.

"So, it's been quite the week," Jenni concluded.

"You can say that again," responded Caitlin. "First, congratulations on the sponsorship. That's awesome, and I'm proud of you, although not surprised. But more importantly, what are you thinking and feeling?"

Jenni took a sip of her wine and paused a moment before answering.

She could try to bluff Caitlin, but Caitlin knew her far too well. And she'd called her so that she could try to sort out her feelings, so she might as well be honest.

"I'm not sure," Jenni shared. "I'm really not in any frame of mind to think about another guy. I did want to be with him. But I did have to teach, and I guess I sounded pretty cold, and maybe even rude, when I told him. Caitlin, I think about him all the time, but I'm just not ready. And hey, an offer to go for a drink might have just been a drink. So, it's not like he's ready to ask me to make a life-long commitment. But he's so perfect, or so it seems, and there's got to be a catch. I can't risk getting hurt again. I just won't go there."

"Jenni, no one is perfect, and we both know that," said Caitlin. "But there are nice guys in the world. Really nice ones. With little faults here and there. But that is what makes them attractive and worth it. They aren't all Compys."

"I know, I know," sighed Jenni as she stood up and started pacing the room. "At first, I hoped we'd be working together, then I was disappointed. But now I'm kind of relieved we're not. I'm all mixed up. But I have to admit, I'm really looking forward to the gala. My time to shine and all that."

"And you will shine," Caitlin assured her. "This will really be a feather in your cap."

They chatted a bit longer, and by the time they ended the call, Jenni felt a little better about everything and even allowed herself to bask in her big achievement of the week.

She poured another glass of wine. Having lost interest in the show she was watching she began to channel surf. She came upon an obscure sports channel featuring, of all things, a saltwater fishing show.

She started to move past it but decided to watch for a bit. Now that the last week was in the rear-view mirror, she could actually think about the fishing part of it in a different light.

It hadn't been all bad. In fact, she had found it some-what exhilarating once she got over her nerves.

She remembered her Uncle Ron vacationing with the family when she was a little girl. He never missed an Outer

Banks vacation. Up before the sun, he'd fish until breakfast and more often than not would have something to show for it.

He'd often tried to encourage her to pick up a rod and try it, but it never held any interest for her. Moreover, since her dad wasn't an angler, she'd never taken up the hobby. Clearly, as she learned from Barb, May Ellen, and Caitlin, in addition to all the other women she'd seen on the beach, women anglers were plentiful.

It certainly got you outdoors and close to nature. Maybe too close when you had to handle bait. But more than that was the closeness to the ocean, breathing the salt air, and watching the sun dance on the waves. Maybe she'd been too quick to cast aside any thoughts of her taking up the sport.

She drained her glass and laughed at the pun she'd made. Maybe, just maybe, after the gala was over and she could make some plans for the summer, she'd pay Uncle Ron a visit and see if he could give her some pointers. Wouldn't he be surprised?

Jenni set her glass in the sink and made her way to bed. As she lay there, she felt calmer than she had in months.

She knew the weeks ahead would be insanely busy but would also fly by. Best to get some good sleep in now, and thankfully she did.

Chapter Thirteen

In the weeks that followed, sleep did indeed become a precious commodity. Jenni's thoughts were full of the gala all day and all night. She had planned and executed several special events in the past, and they'd all turned out reasonably well, but the stakes were higher for this event, both personally as well as professionally.

She found that getting an uninterrupted night's sleep was almost an impossibility. Lists upon lists of things to do rattled around in her brain at all hours of the night. The pencil and pad she kept by her bed were used more than once to capture a thought she was afraid she'd forget by morning.

The staff at *Raleigh Wins* was small, and she didn't have many helping hands besides her own to take care of the myriad responsibilities.

She met with the caterers, talked to the printers, worked with the staff at the venue for all of the audio-visual needs, kept spreadsheets of who was attending, and worked on collecting and organizing the silent auction gifts. The running of the auction was no small feat in and of itself. She knew that much larger organizations were now using all sorts of hand-held devices and even phone apps for auctions, but she and Dee were trying to keep the costs down to maximize their final return.

Dee had been in and out of the office tending to donor requests, but she was also being pulled away from time to time to tend to her mother.

Jenni's heart ached for her, and she was so thankful that for now, her own parents were doing just fine. She realized she hadn't spent much time with them at all recently and vowed to make amends during the summer.

Apex was really a suburb of Raleigh, and so it should have been easy enough to catch up with them, but they were leading busy lives and so was she.

Still, when she saw Dee, she knew she had to do a better job of not just texting but actually calling or better yet, visiting her parents.

All that being said, it meant she was putting in a ton of hours and felt tired all the time. As expected, she and Tory were in almost constant communication.

Jenni admitted to herself they were almost friends now. In fact, they were.

Jenni was also keeping up with her teaching responsibilities, and those demands never ended as well. But she believed in what she was doing, and it would take more than a gala to make her stop.

It also gave her a convenient excuse when Caleb texted again.

Hey Jenni! How about drinks on Wednesday after work? Are you free this time?

Sorry Caleb, but I honestly can't make it. ☹

She thought, and honestly hoped, the sad face emoji would ease the sting. She hadn't heard from him since.

When she and Jenni talked, Tory indicated Caleb had been very busy. Apparently, Mr. Ragland's illness had turned into much more than anyone had anticipated, so Caleb, as well as the other vice presidents on the bank staff, were picking up his responsibilities as best they could. Jenni was careful not to ask Tory about Caleb, but Tory often volunteered information.

The event was a week or so away when she and Tory decided to take a break and have lunch together. Tory had stepped up to help Jenni in ways beyond anything that related to the sponsorship, and she felt she needed to show her gratitude.

It was a warm May lunch hour when they met and decided to sit at an outside table to enjoy the springtime air before it turned stifling hot in the summer.

"So, how are your numbers looking?" asked Tory as she perused the menu. "Both in terms of attendees and potential fund raising, if it's ok to ask."

Jenni quickly scanned her menu and, settling on something pretty quickly, she responded, "Right now, I'm holding my breath because everything looks fantastic. We are at three hundred guests and that's far more than we've ever had. I'm glad that my boss insisted we book a larger venue. Based on the sponsorships alone we are looking at about twenty-five thousand dollars, and once you add in the ticket prices, silent auction, raffle tickets, and the like, we might clear forty thousand which would be incredible."

Tory's eyes widened. "That is incredible. I know what some of the large, really large charities do, and it's difficult to compete with that, but for your size organization, you can really feel good about things. I know Mr. Prescott will be impressed." She looked up and seemed to be waiting for Jenni to respond.

At that moment, the server came to take their orders, so Jenni had a slight reprieve, but she again realized that Tory didn't miss a trick.

Jenni just smiled and said, "Well, that's important. We always want our sponsors to be pleased. And speaking of that, we really need to discuss your table arrangements. You'll want the full table of eight that comes with the sponsorship, correct?"

Tory nodded and sipped on her water. "There will be two other VPs and their wives since Mr. Ragland can't make it, I'll be there with my boyfriend, and then Mr. Prescott and his plus one."

Jenni expected that Tory wanted her to ask about the "plus one," but she held her tongue. The news, however, gave her a very bad feeling in the pit of her stomach. She recovered enough to say, "That's good to know, Tory. I'm looking forward to meeting your boyfriend. Chase, isn't it?"

Tory grinned, and Jenni felt she had successfully shifted the conversation away from Caleb for the moment. Tory gushed about Chase's new job and his apartment and dog for several minutes, so much so, that by the time she'd exhausted those subjects, their food had arrived.

They chatted about inconsequential things, but Jenni couldn't help but wonder who Caleb would be bringing to the event. It was none of her business, of course. She had turned him down twice, but she wondered anyway.

She was surprised that it hurt.

As they paid their respective bills and turned to go back to their offices, Tory added, "You know, Mr. Prescott says he is really looking forward to this event. He usually doesn't care much about these kinds of things. He goes to so many."

Again, she seemed to expect some sort of reply from Jenni, but Jenni just said, "Well, I hope he won't be disappointed. We all have worked so hard, and of course that includes you. You've been a rock star."

Tory smiled and waved goodbye, leaving Jenni to feel more confused by the moment. So, he's bringing a plus one, but he's very excited about the event? Again, she tried to sort out her feelings, but she realized she just couldn't, so she headed back to the office feeling very out of sorts and unsettled.

Those feelings continued to plague her as the big day approached, and she slowly started to understand that she truly wanted to impress Caleb Prescott.

Chapter Fourteen

By the time that Thursday came, the day of the actual event, she was more excited than ever.

She tried not to dwell on the plus one and rationalized it in every possible way she could. Maybe there was another assistant somewhere, or that classy receptionist in the lobby, who needed to be rewarded for some reason. But Tory said he was excited to attend, and that was all that mattered to her.

She spent the morning and the early afternoon at the venue. Dee finally ordered her to go home and get cleaned up so that she could arrive an hour before things got underway.

"I just want to be sure everything is perfect," she stressed to Dee, once again counting tables and place settings although the venue staff obviously knew how to count to three hundred.

"I know that, but I need you fresh for this evening. I think we have done everything here we possibly can, and it looks great. Did I mention to you that at the close of the evening I want you to thank the sponsors? That's an appropriate thing for you to do, and it will really put your face out there for the organization. It's a small thing but an important one."

Jenni knew she should thank Dee for the opportunity, which she did, but inwardly, she was less than enthusiastic. She had hoped just to remain on the fringes of everything.

Gala events are great fun for attendees. But staffing one, being responsible for one, is a tremendous amount of work. She'd have to remember to bring an extra pair of shoes so that when she stepped up to the podium, she'd look like the professional she was supposed to be and not the exhausted party planner she felt like. Normally, she'd just wear flats.

Jenni had dithered over what she was going to wear, and she still hadn't made a decision when she stepped out of the shower. She had thought about a very chic jumpsuit, but at the last minute, she went for the classic little black dress. She'd lost enough weight over the past year that the dress fit her like a glove, and with her grandmother's pearls and a pair of high black heels, she felt classy and elegant. She would definitely throw in some black slip-ons for that hour before everyone arrived and for clean-up. But for the big event, she would wow them all.

Dee was the first to notice when Jenni walked back into the venue at half past five.

"Well, look at you. You're like the butterfly that emerged from the cocoon," Dee exclaimed. "Jenni, you look lovely."

"Thank you, I guess," she said as she feigned a sad look. "I didn't know I've been looking like a caterpillar recently."

"That's not what I meant," Dee said. "I'm just pleased to see you getting excited about life. When you first came to us, I honestly wasn't sure you'd come out of that self-imposed shell you put yourself in. I'm glad I was wrong."

Jenni hugged her and began the final checklist before the onslaught of guests. There were always people who came a bit early, and she was there to greet them along with Dee, encouraging them to have a glass of champagne and to bid on the silent auction items. Soon, the guests were arriving in droves. Jenni quickly remembered to switch shoes, shoving the flats under her seat, and taking a moment to scan the crowd. She hoped she remembered how to walk in heels.

It was quite a bit later that she saw Tory waving to her and bringing the young man who was obviously Chase to meet her. She and Tory hugged, and they both exclaimed how fabulous the other looked. Chase held onto Tory like a prized possession, and Jenni was sure to tell him how much she enjoyed working with her and how Second Bank was lucky to have her.

"Speaking of the bank," she said to Tory. "Where are your colleagues?"

"Oh, they're here somewhere. Probably bidding on things. It's a thing at the office the day after a gala event. It's like a competition to see who scored the best item." Tory paused for a moment and then said in a rush, "Um, Mr.

Prescott isn't here yet. He'll probably get here late. He got hung up with something, he didn't say what. I just got a text from him."

Jenni pretended this piece of news was of no interest to her, but she felt her spirit sink. Tory did say late and not that he *wasn't* coming, she reminded herself. But she had hoped to at least say hello before the meal and program got underway. Well, there was always right after everything ended, but she'd be busy then.

She spoke to several more guests, and soon it was time for everyone to take their seats.

From where Jenni sat at her table, the podium blocked her view of the Second Bank group. She thought she could make out the tops of the heads of Tory and Chase, and apparently the two other couples, but no one else, and clearly no Caleb. She reluctantly turned her attention to the board members seated next to her and politely made the necessary small talk while dinner was served and the program got underway.

No matter how many times Jenni worked on a special event, it always amazed her how quickly the evening would pass after months and months of preparation. This evening was no different.

She tried to be in the moment to remember what she ate for dinner, the motivational words of the keynote speaker, and the outline of the future plans of the organization from Dee who was delivering the closing remarks.

She was jolted out of her reverie when she heard Dee conclude by saying, "These wonderful evenings don't just happen by themselves. I am sure you will want to join me in thanking Jenni Kirk, our development director, for all her hard work to make this evening such a resounding success.

To close out our program, I'd like Jenni to come up and again thank our sponsors."

Jenni stood and walked to the podium. She noticed two things immediately.

First, there was no piece of paper, no list of sponsors, awaiting her on the podium. Was she to have prepared them and forgot to do so? But it was the second thing she noticed that made her heart stop and her blood run cold. At the Second Bank table, Caleb had obviously arrived, with the most beautiful woman Jenni had ever seen.

She was so taken aback it took her a moment to regain her composure. And then she again remembered she had no list.

Not knowing what else to do, she looked over to Dee and said, "Dee, did you happen to pick up the list? I'm sure I could recite it, but I wouldn't want to make a mistake."

She thought she could sense a bit of a nervous titter settle over the audience and she felt her face grow hot with embarrassment.

She could not look Caleb in the eye.

Dee looked through her papers and laughed, "Here it is!" She waved it enthusiastically as she brought it up to Jenni. "You're good, but memorizing this list wasn't expected." The crowd laughed.

Chapter Fifteen

Jenni's mouth was dry, and her hands were shaking, but she carefully read through each sponsor's name and allowed for applause. Finally, she'd reached the last name.

"And of course, we want to acknowledge the wonderful contribution from Second Bank as our presenting sponsor. Would the bank representatives please rise to be thanked appropriately?"

Tory, the two other gentlemen, and Caleb rose while the crowd clapped and even cheered a bit. When Caleb sat down, Jenni noticed the woman touch him lightly on the arm and ruffle his hair playfully.

Jenni felt faint and was barely able to, once again, thank everyone and wish them a good evening. Once it was clear the evening was over, chairs were pushed back and the volume of noise in the room escalated. Controlled chaos was exactly what Jenni needed. She turned from the podium, kicked off her heels as she passed her table, and made her way through the crowd. She practically ran barefoot into the ladies' room and threw herself into a stall.

She sobbed uncontrollably.

But of course, he had a date, she chastised herself. *And of course, I had to screw up again. When he is around, I can't do anything right.*

It should have been me on his arm tonight. He didn't need a plus one. I had my chances, and I blew them. Over and over. Then he looked elsewhere.

I just should have known. I should have prepared myself for this.

He is an amazing guy. Why would he wait around for me to figure out that it's him I really want, but I'm too fearful to tell him?

Why am I still so afraid of being hurt again?

Jenni sat there, with her head in her hands, tears streaming down her face, for several minutes. Then she realized she had things to do.

If nothing else Dee would be looking for her. She got up and went to the sink splashing cold water on her face, when Tory walked in.

"Jenni, what are you doing in here? I've been trying to find you. It was such a great night and... What on earth is wrong?"

Jenni shook her head as if to say it was nothing. "I think I must have eaten something that didn't agree with me. Had to run, you know?" She hoped Tory would accept the story.

If Tory was skeptical, thankfully, she didn't appear to let on.

"I just wanted to say congratulations. You'll have to let me know your end result. Chase is in line to pick up a silent auction item for Mr. Prescott. Lucky him, Mr. Prescott that is, he got the golf package at Pinehurst. He had to leave right away, and well, you know, the assistant takes care of everything. Anyway, he was looking for you, and said if I found you, to congratulate you too."

"Oh, thanks," Jenni mumbled. "I guess I'd better get out there and do my job."

Tory looked a bit puzzled by the tone of Jenni's response, so Jenni retreated. "I'm sorry, Tory. Didn't mean for that to come out like that. I think I am just overtired now and can't really take it all in. I think I just need to sleep for days."

As they walked out together, Jenni felt as if she was sick.

Just hearing Caleb's name again and knowing that he didn't wait to say hello, even if it meant her coming face-to-face with his date for the night, made her unbelievably sad.

She knew she had wanted to talk to him and hear his congratulations herself.

Now she never would. And it was all her fault.

Again.

Dee ran up to them. "Jenni, I was looking for you, you look pale."

"I'm fine," responded Jenni, thankful to know Caleb was no longer on the premises. "Just a bit of a wonky tummy. Too much excitement, I guess, especially with that list and all."

"So sorry about that," Dee said. Putting her hands on Jenni's shoulders. "But you handled it with, what's the word? Aplomb. What a great night! I don't expect you in tomorrow. I hope you know that. We'll clean up here, and I will see you on Monday."

Jenni said good night again to Tory and a few others, then busied herself with the clean-up, happy that the crowd cleared out quickly.

She picked up her program, her purse, and her strappy black shoes, and placed the sensible flats firmly on her feet for the walk out to her car.

It was a warm night, and summer was definitely in the air. She sat in her car for a long time, trying not to cry but eventually letting the tears flow freely even as she put the car in gear and made the drive home.

She had waited too long to acknowledge her feelings about Caleb Prescott. She knew that. But he was unavailable and now that the gala was over, she wouldn't have to worry about him again. Best to focus on the next project.

Too bad summer was always a slow time for them at work.

She'd come up with something. She had to.

She pulled into her apartment parking lot, opened her door, and stood looking at the few stars she could see, given the light pollution of the city.

Hatteras has so many stars, she thought. *I want to see them again.*

Chapter Sixteen

May melted into June as the memories of the gala, while still raw, were at least tolerable in Jenni's mind.

Assuming she was at fault for everything that had happened was a sensation she'd become used to. She just lived with it.

After a few weeks, she decided to leave Raleigh if only for a day or two.

She was now sharing an early morning cup of coffee with her mom.

Remembering the vow she'd made to visit her parents in

person, she had arrived last night after work and decided to spend the night.

Her parents lived in Apex, a well-kept Raleigh suburb. Not quite a retirement community, but it wasn't the house she had grown up in. They had downsized a few years earlier and as far as Jenni could tell had settled easily into a new neighborhood and had made new friends.

Jenni had planned to spend the Independence Day holiday with them, but two things happened to, once again, rearrange her plans.

"So, you and Dad are really headed off to Texas for the fourth?" she asked as she and her mom rocked in unison on the front porch. "I never thought you'd get Dad traveling over a holiday. How did you twist his arm?"

"Grandchildren." Her mom winked. "When your sister mentioned that the kids were old enough to enjoy all the festivities, and especially the fireworks, your father was totally on board. You know he loves those kids to bits, but he's been waiting for them to grow up."

Her mom took a bite out of the ham, egg, and cheese biscuit she'd carried out from the kitchen. "He wants to do grandfather things with them. I guess now, at five and seven, it's time. He's more comfortable with them now than he was when they were just babies and toddlers. Plus, we haven't seen them in almost a year, and on the last visit, they drove all the way here."

Jenni remembered her sister practically collapsing after that road trip and vowing she wasn't going to travel with the kids ever again. At least for this visit, she would get her wish.

Her mother, Rachel, handed Jenni the plate of biscuits, and Jenni took one.

Then her mom stopped rocking for a moment and

looked at Jenni directly. "I know you had said something about us getting together, so if you'd like to fly to Texas, you're certainly welcome to join us.

Jenni smiled. "No, this should be a grandparents' delight." She laughed. "And believe it or not, Caitlin texted me just the other day with an invitation to go back to Hatteras. I really think I could use the break."

What she didn't say was that visiting with her young niece and nephew was not the kind of break she had in mind.

Her mom took the news in stride. "That's great, hon," she said. "Given what you've told me about the gala, I know you've earned a bit of time away."

"Well, honestly, the office is going to close for the week," Jenni said as she stretched her legs blissfully. "Since the holiday is on Thursday, Dee said it didn't make sense to come in, go out, and come back. There's absolutely nothing going on, and I think Dee will use that week to move her mom to a facility with a more intense level of care. Her mom isn't doing well at all."

Mom nodded. "Sorry to hear that but glad you'll have a nice week to relax. Caitlin's mom and dad both going?"

"Yes," answered Jenni. "And I think Andrew will be there as well. This will certainly be a different kind of trip from the one I made in April. But who knows, I just might pick up a rod and see what I can catch in the heat of the summer."

"You know you really should catch up with Uncle Ron sometime," said Rachel. "He can give you a lot of pointers. And he'd get such a big kick out of it."

"You're right, I should," agreed Jenni as she got up from her chair. "Now let me help you with the breakfast dishes and give Dad a hug before I head back home. Y'all have a wonderful trip and give the fam my love. I'll get out there one of these days."

On the drive home, she decided to give her Uncle Ron a call in the next week or so before she left for the coast. Probably not enough time to pay him a visit, as he lived close to Asheville, but she could at least chat with him a bit.

Her mom was absolutely correct. When Jenni called, he sounded thrilled to talk to her and equally thrilled that she wanted information about surf fishing. He explained that in the heat of the summer, not too many fish were biting, not like the big schools in the spring or fall, but there was always something interesting to catch. And if she could get offshore just to experience the Gulf Stream and catch a few fish out there like tuna or dolphin, well, that would be fantastic.

Now, a few short weeks later, Jenni was headed out of Raleigh and on her way to the Outer Banks.

She laughed at the memory of telling her uncle she would in no way ever even want to catch a dolphin, when he patiently explained that he didn't mean the bottle-nose mammal type, but the fish otherwise known as mahi-mahi. She had told him she doubted if she'd have a chance to do that, but she thanked him, nonetheless.

The difference between traveling east in April and July was startling. It seemed as though Raleigh had been evacuated and all roads led to the OBX, the popular shorthand for the Outer Banks.

She noted license plates from all over the east coast and plenty from further afield. For a moment, she wondered if Caleb would be there, somewhere in the throngs of vacationers, but she tried not to dwell on the subject.

He had texted her a few times after the gala event, but

Jenni had this strange sense of betrayal she couldn't shake, and she chose not to respond.

She remembered one time in particular.

Hi Jenni!

I'd love to talk to you about the gala. Just say when!

☺

She deleted it line by line until all that was left was the smile emoji.

It was still on her phone. She just couldn't delete it.

He never tried to call, thankfully, and the few times she'd spoken to Tory since then, his name wasn't mentioned by either one of them.

This time, when she made it to Whalebone Junction, she remembered to pull in and text Caitlin. She was startled at how difficult it was even to make a right-hand turn as she rejoined the steady line of traffic headed south on Highway 12. The light was so different.

She left Raleigh before sunrise to avoid the traffic. And now, even though it was still relatively early in the day, the sun was intense. She felt like she was baking in her car, despite the air conditioning working perfectly.

From the top of the new Basnight Bridge, the ocean just shimmered, and the sky was a brilliant blue. But glancing to the west, she noticed the beginnings of clouds building, a pretty sure sign that thunderstorms would pop up by the afternoon.

She habitually held her breath driving over the top and then relaxed and exhaled as she drove down the other side, wondering just how many people crossing the bridge did the same thing.

She was looking forward to seeing Caitlin and Andrew.

Knowing they would want time alone together would give her the chance to do what she'd wanted to do in April, just relax.

She also knew she'd love talking to Barb, and Caitlin's dad, Scott. She was spending the better part of the week with them, and she was certain there would be a lot of reminiscing about her and Caitlin's college days. She hoped Barb wouldn't talk too much about all that had transpired back in April. Those memories, along with what had happened more recently, were still very painful for Jenni.

While the traffic was nearly bumper to bumper, and the speeds were slow in the villages she passed through along the way, she still made good time and arrived at the "Mermaid's Mansion" just a little over an hour after she'd texted Caitlin.

Chapter Seventeen

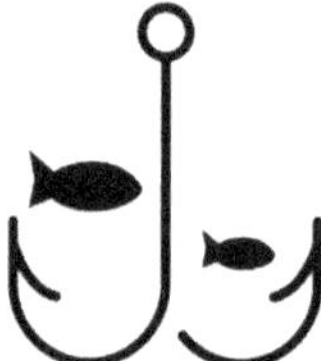

Caitlin's dad was up under the house doing something with a garden hose as she pulled into the drive. He set it down and came over to greet her with a big bear hug as soon as she stepped out of her car.

"Hi, Scott."

"Jenni, glad to have you here," he said. "Did you have much trouble on the drive? It's been a mad house here for the past several days. Every year I think it can't get any more crowded and then, somehow it is."

"Plenty of traffic for sure, but it kept moving," Jenni replied as she pulled her suitcase from her hatchback.

She was surprised no one else had come out to greet her.

Scott grabbed her case and said, "I'll take that up for you. Caitlin and Andrew and Barb just zipped over to the Sunshine Mart for a few things, so make yourself at home. I think you have the same room that you had in April."

Jenni unpacked and poured herself a glass of iced tea while she waited for their return. She scanned her phone's weather app and saw that summer thunderstorms notwithstanding, it would be "hotter than a firecracker," as her dad would say, for the entire week.

When she heard a car pull into the driveway, she walked out onto the porch and waved.

Caitlin waved back and kept waving and waving until Jenni got the glint of something in the sun.

"Oh, my God," she screamed and ran down the steps. "Let me see that!"

She grabbed Caitlin's left hand and looked at the gorgeous diamond sparkling just like she'd seen the ocean water sparkle on brilliantly sunny days.

She hugged her friend and then turned to hug Andrew and then Barb and then Scott in turn.

"When?" Jenni asked breathlessly.

"A few nights ago, actually right before we left to come up here," Caitlin said. She stared at the ring as though she thought it might disappear. "I was totally shocked, although Dad already knew." She looked at Scott and beamed. "Andrew actually called and asked him for my hand." She laughed. "How cool is that?"

Jenni looked at Barb, who, probably not for the first time, had tears in her eyes. "How does it feel to be a MOB?" Jenni asked.

"A what?" said Barb, looking confused.

"Mother of the bride," Jenni clarified. "You've got big responsibilities, you know?"

Barb grabbed a bag of groceries and started up the stairs. "I expect you to help me. I've heard all about your party-planning skills, Ms. Kirk. And since…" Her voice suddenly trailed off.

Now it was Jenni's turn to look confused. Caitlin looked a bit exasperated, but she shrugged and said, "Well, Mom, you almost spilled the beans, but now is as good a time as any, I suppose. Jenni, how does MOH sound to you? As in maid of honor?"

Jenni gasped and hugged her friend all over again. "Of course, CayCay, you know it will be my honor."

Barb, who had made it up the stairs, called down from the railing, "Please, bring the rest of those groceries up before they cook right there. Jenni, I hope you're hungry, we bought enough to feed an army. But it's time for a little cele-bration, so why don't we head to Marcie's for lunch and plan out these next few days?"

Groceries put up, Jenni rode with Caitlin and Andrew, with Barb and Scott following close behind. Jenni had a million questions about the wedding and how many deci-sions they had already made. They talked incessantly and were still at it when Andrew pulled into the lot at Marcie's.

"We're a bit early for lunch," admitted Caitlin, "But at least we'll get a seat."

She then turned to Jenni and spoke in a whisper. "Have you seen or heard from Caleb?"

Jenni shook her head.

She felt that same sick feeling in the pit of her stomach but tried to keep her voice emotionless. "No, and it's prob-ably better that way. I wonder if he's using his golf package at Pinehurst this weekend?"

Caitlin said nothing, and Jenni was relieved. Hopefully, Caitlin sensed that Caleb was not a good topic.

Andrew held the door for them as they walked into the restaurant, and Caitlin immediately spotted Chris and Susan Smith, Mike and SeaAnna Leornard, and JoBell Leonard. "Let's go sit by them," she suggested.

They all rose and exchanged greetings. JoBell smiled warmly at Jenni as they were introduced. "My mom told me you went to St. Adrian's too. I have to say my years there were challenging. I think I enjoy the memories much more than I enjoyed the school when I was there."

Jenni nodded. "Agreed. But it seemed it gave you a great start for your college career. I told Caitlin and your mom I've seen several articles about you in the alumni magazine."

JoBell blushed as Scott and Barb caught up with the group. "Let's push these tables together so we can all talk," Barb suggested.

Marcie welcomed them all and brought over a few more menus.

Lunch was underway in no time.

JoBell was seated next to Jenni, and they shared a few stories about their school days and how things had changed from Jenni's time to JoBell's. Then JoBell changed the subject.

"What are your plans for the next few days?" she asked Jenni.

Jenni looked at Caitlin and shrugged. "I literally just got here maybe an hour ago, so we haven't discussed it. Enjoy the beach, I suspect, and eat until we burst."

JoBell laughed. "I have a proposition. Tomorrow is the third, and for once, Dare decided that he would take me and my family out for a day in the Gulf Stream. However," she said, casting a glance at Chris, Susan, and SeaAnna, "Gran,

Chris, and Mom have decided to bail. Too hot for them. Dad is going as he's become Dare's trusty mate on special occasions." She paused, and Mike nodded solemnly.

"He couldn't manage without me," he said seriously and then laughed. "He'll put up with me, that's about the size of it."

"That leaves plenty of room," Jo continued. "Andrew, Caitlin, Jenni, would you like to come? It's a full day but with the weather this calm, it should be incredible, and I know, well, I think I know you'd enjoy it."

Jenni knew that Andrew and Caitlin would agree to go anywhere as long as they were together, and she didn't want to be a third wheel, but since Mike, JoBell, and obviously Dare would be there too, why not go? Maybe she could learn a few things to share with Uncle Ron.

She looked at Caitlin and listened to Andrew who was in the middle of saying, "Are you kidding? Going to the Gulf Stream is a bucket list item for me. We'd love to go, right, Caitlin?"

Caitlin nodded happily and looked expectantly at Jenni. "You're in, right? I know it seems I'm always changing your plans, but this will be fun!"

Jenni didn't disagree. She thought back to her conversation with her uncle and knew she'd really surprise him with tales of this adventure. She nodded affirmatively to the group. "I am absolutely in."

For the next hour while Barb, Scott, Chris, Susan, and SeaAnna talked about the latest island happenings and gossip, Mike slid his chair closer to the younger set and discussed what the day trip involved.

"I've gone out with Dare a few times now." He smiled before frowning.

He admonished, "Whatever you do, don't forget your

sunscreen and a hat. He usually keeps water in the cooler, but I think it's wise if you bring your own. And anything else you want to drink or eat."

He looked at each of us in turn. "Jo, I know you're good out on the water, but do any of the three of you get seasick? It's going to be calm, but some people can't even take that."

He looked around, and when no one seemed to have any issues, he said, "I'll let Jo tell you the really fun part. Like what time we'll be leaving."

Jo playfully shoved her dad's shoulder. "It gets light so early, hopefully you won't really mind, but we need to be down at the docks and ready to get on board the SeaAnna Two at about six. Which probably means a wake-up call at five. Is that OK?"

Jenni looked at Caitlin and laughed. "Oh, you so owe me, again."

With a few more questions answered, the group disbanded with waves and promises from the fishing party to regroup at the dock early in the morning.

Back at the house, Jenni looked over at Caitlin and said, "I can't believe that we're going out tomorrow. This place never ceases to amaze me. I guess I'll try my hand at offshore fishing. My uncle won't believe it. In fact, I'm not believing it, but if my April experience taught me anything it's to be flexible and take what Hatteras gives you."

Chapter Eighteen

The docks were already humming with activity when Jenni, Caitlin, and Andrew pulled into one of the few remaining parking spaces the next morning.

"It's like when I fly," remarked Andrew. "You think you're the only person in the world who would be getting up this early, but there are plenty of people who do it all the time."

Jenni nodded as she took in all the sights and sounds.

There was a smell, a mixture of diesel and bait and salt air that was hard to explain but unmistakable.

The three walked along until they spotted Mike and Jo, and someone who was obviously Dare tending to the SeaAnna II.

Mike looked up and waved. "Right on time," he said as he adjusted some ropes along the dock.

Jenni was overcome with everything she saw. This was a different kind of fishing than what she had experienced back in April. Noticing her fascination, Mike remarked, "This is what it's like in the middle of the busy season. These folks are all paying a premium for a day offshore. They've all got dreams of marlin and sailfish and the like. We'll probably see many of these same boats once we're out there, especially if we start catching fish."

Dare had been up in the tower, but now he came down the ladder, onto the dock, exchanging introductions and shaking hands with everyone. "I know I'm crazy for taking my almost-family out in the middle of the tourist season, but I made these plans a long time ago. When Susan, Chris, and SeaAnna said they just weren't up to it in this heat, I was going to take some make-up folks...um, those are people who don't have a full party but will go along with others in the same, well, the same boat."

They all laughed.

He continued, "But then Jo made the invite. She gave me the heads-up, and here you are. I am glad it worked out. Andrew, I hear this is a bucket list trip for you. Don't hesitate to ask me questions and..." he said glancing around at everyone, "Jo and Mike can answer a fair amount too. And if we see jellies, Jo will go nuts."

He looked over at Jo, and she nodded in full agreement. "I will," she promised.

Dare began to assist them one by one onto the boat. Jo

and Mike hopped on unassisted. Jenni noted that while Mike was becoming more experienced with how to help Dare, he deferred to him, asking him questions and following instructions.

"Do you mate often?" Jenni asked.

"Dare's normal first mate wanted to spend the day with his family, so I volunteered," Mike said. "I certainly don't know everything, but Dare is great at telling me what to do."

"I sure am," Dare grinned, then turned to the group. "One more thing, I don't normally fish offshore. Inshore is my thing. But with today being what we call 'slick cam,' it won't be an issue. Hardly any wind, not much in the way of waves. The only thing is, it's going to be really hot out there, so I've made sure we have lots of water. Hope y'all brought hats."

They all nodded, but Jenni was still thinking about what Dare had just said. "Don't you mean calm?" she asked.

Dare smiled. "Nope, down here it's slick cam. Use that phrase, and you'll almost be mistaken for a native. Now, have a seat, it's about an hour and a half to the Gulf Stream. Just relax, enjoy the early morning cool, and we're off."

He scampered up the tower with Jo right behind him. Caitlin and Andrew were seated on one side, so Jenni decided she'd sit on the other while Mike was busy preparing rigs and checking on bait.

Every boat was obviously on the same time schedule, so they all made their way out of the harbor and into the sound in a convoy of sorts.

"Do we all just go in a big line?" she asked Mike.

"More or less until we get out of the inlet," Mike answered. "There is so much shoaling that the channels are ridiculously narrow. Some of the boats can cut across, but you have to know what you're doing and be a relatively small boat. You'll see the ferries using the channel as well. It will take us nearly as long to get out into the ocean as it will to get to the famous Gulf Stream current."

Jenni sat back and let the wind from the movement of the boat rush through her hair. She grabbed a ponytail band she'd placed on her wrist and pulled her hair up. She knew it wasn't done perfectly but she also knew that when you fished, you didn't get points for your fashion sense. Some boats were able to pass by them as they headed out, folks waving or shouting as they zoomed by.

She swore she saw Caleb on board another boat, but she also knew she had an overactive imagination.

Her heart raced.

She realized to her dismay that the more she tried to forget about him, the more she thought about him.

If he really was here, would she see him? She shook her head as if to shake away the thoughts, but it didn't work.

She knew she longed to see him, even if it was from a distance.

As they made their way through the inlet, she found herself deep in thought, observing the two couples on her boat. When she craned her neck and looked up, she could see Jo and Dare sitting side by side on the tower, their blue-green polarized sunglasses glinting in the rising sun.

They seemed to be talking non-stop with Dare pointing to other boats or chatting on the radio, and Jo gesturing, obviously adding her thoughts. Jenni couldn't hear anything clearly, but she could sense they were very comfortable with each other.

She remembered that she had heard somewhere, maybe it was back in April, that the two had grown up together in the summers when Jo visited her grandmother, and then later worked at her motel. But she'd also heard they weren't really a couple.

Who's fooling who on that one? she thought. *They seem like a couple to me.*

Chapter Nineteen

The slight rocking of the boat was very soothing, and Caitlin and Andrew looked like they were asleep, her head on his shoulder.

Jenni knew their story far better. When Caitlin met Andrew in Charleston, it was the old love at first sight thing, but they dated for several years before they moved in together. Caitlin admitted that there were things about Andrew she would never have known had they not spent so much time together, and the same held true for him.

According to her, learning those things in advance

helped them shape their relationship and work through some rough patches.

With Compy, Jenni wasn't sure if it was love or just infatuation. He was everything she'd dreamed of, or so she thought, and marrying immediately after graduation, she really didn't know what made him tick.

She felt she was responsible for so much of the failure of their marriage, but realistically she knew that he had to accept some blame as well.

The thing was, he never did. He blamed Jenni, and she took all the blame.

Then, humiliated and scarred, she escaped back to Raleigh. She never tried to fight to get him back, but now, upon reflection, maybe it was a good thing she hadn't.

"Penny for your thoughts," said Mike as he moved to sit down next to her. "Or would you rather be alone?"

"No, it's fine, Mike. Thanks. I guess being out here really sets your mind free," Jenni said as she accepted a bottle of water Mike offered.

"That's true," he agreed. "At least for me. So, you're a St. Adrian's grad too. Tell me about yourself."

Jenni began with the basics. Mike was a good listener, and soon she surprisingly found herself sharing about Compy, the fishing tournament, and even a bit about the gala.

She tried to be very circumspect when mentioning Caleb, but Mike was very astute.

"SeaAnna always chastises me for trying to be an amateur psychologist," Mike began when Jenni concluded her sharing. "But I see several things going on. Maybe you've already thought about them or maybe not. Would you like for me to go on?"

Jenni nodded and took a drink of water. They were out

in the ocean now, moving quickly, but even the wind couldn't provide enough cooling. It was going to be hot.

"I know your ex-husband hurt you deeply, but it seems you've allowed him to become the model for all men. SeaAnna would be the first one to tell you my faults." He smiled. "But we're not all like your ex. So, you have to give people a chance."

Mike paused for a moment before continuing. "There's a funny saying, probably a meme on Facebook or something, that says there's a reason the windshield is bigger than the rearview mirror. At some point, you have to let go of the past and not let it define your future. Susan, Jo's grandmother, went through a big hurt with Chris, and they almost lost what they have today. I don't know what turned her around, but I do know it took a lot of self-work and soul-searching on her part. Thankfully, for our family, I can say it has had a very happy ending."

He shifted on the seat and caught a signal from Dare. "There are a few more things I need to do before we get ready to fish. Hope I didn't stick my nose in where it doesn't belong."

"You didn't at all," said Jenni, adjusting her hat in the wind. "Lots to think about for sure."

"Right now, let's think about fish," he said as he stood up. "That will clear your head."

Jenni could see that while the cavalcade of boats had spread out somewhat since they'd hit the open ocean, they were still relatively close.

Suddenly, she noticed a change in the color of the water and she swore that somehow, they'd made it to the Caribbean. Caitlin and Andrew, who had ended their morning nap, were equally in awe.

"Gulf Stream," shouted Dare. "And I'm hearing some chatter about tuna."

"Do all the boats talk to one another?" asked Caitlin.

"Absolutely," laughed Mike. "You should hear some of the nonsense they discuss. But they also are all friends and competitors, so when a boat starts catching fish, everyone knows it, and it's immediately a game of one-upmanship."

He motioned to Jenni. "Do you want to sit in the chair?"

Jenni shook her head no and looked at Andrew. "This is really meaningful for you. Have at it."

He jumped at the chance, and Mike handed him a rod, and the line and bait disappeared into the boat's wake. Jenni watched as Dare maneuvered the SeaAnna II to where a school of tuna was apparently headed.

Suddenly, Mike, Dare, and Jo all shouted and Andrew lurched forward in the chair. His rod tip was bent down, and he began the try to reel his catch in.

"Keep the tip up," Jo yelled down.

Perspiration was forming on Andrew's forehead, and the muscles in his arms strained. "I had no idea..." he panted.

"Just keep reeling," replied Mike. Dare had come down from the tower to lend a hand, and Jenni was amazed to see Jo guiding the boat as Dare called up instructions. "I don't want you to lose this fish!"

Dare stood over the edge of the boat and pointed for Jenni to look. "There it is. Do you see it now? A nice tuna. Andrew, keep reeling."

Jenni thought Andrew would give up, but he persevered. In a matter of moments, there was a flash of color as Dare leaned over with the gaff and brought the fish onto the deck. The rest of them applauded and Andrew was ecstatic.

"Mike, I think you can take it from here," Dare said as

he scrambled up the tower. He was immediately on the radio, and Jenni knew Andrew's catch was the talk of the moment.

She could see other anglers bringing fish on board their boats as well, so clearly it was starting out to be a good day.

"Nice one, Andrew." Mike patted him on the back. "I wouldn't have known exactly how to gaff that fish, so I'm glad Dare came down. If I'd lost it for you...well, I guess it would be a long swim home."

They all laughed as Caitlin took the requisite photos for social media. Andrew beamed.

"Who wants to be next?" Mike asked, and Caitlin stepped up.

Chapter Twenty

The school of tuna had come and gone, and there were no more tuna caught that day. They did see some amazing jellyfish float by, and Jo happily pointed out the various species and their interesting stories, she being the resident expert on jellies.

They shared lunch and caught a few smaller fish and listened to the chatter from the other boats as the sun passed high overhead.

Jenni learned about the currents, the shipping lanes, and stories of storms and shipwrecks. It felt like they had been on the water just a few hours, so Jenni was shocked when Dare announced that they'd be headed back.

The day had truly flown by.

Jo came down and asked Mike if he'd like to be on the tower with Dare. She sat down next to Jenni and asked how she'd enjoyed the day.

"This was incredible," gasped Jenni. "I feel like I have learned so much. And I did catch one small mackerel, which was fun. I have an uncle who will love hearing about all of this. I can't thank you enough, it was so generous of you to offer. I mean, we're practically strangers. At least, I am."

"Consider it an alumni reunion." Jo laughed. "And having y'all on board made it a lot of fun. I rarely get to go out with Dare, so this time together is special for us. When we were kids, we had all the time in the world. It's different now for sure," she added wistfully.

They sat in silence for a few minutes, Jenni noting that one by one the boats were all more or less in a line again heading back into the inlet.

"Um, Jo, can I ask you a question, a kind of personal one?" Jenni asked.

Jo cocked her head to one side and said carefully, "Sure. Have at it."

"Do you trust Dare?" Jenni blurted out.

Jo looked shocked for a moment and then regained her composure. "Well, of all the things I thought you might ask, that wasn't on my list. But to answer your question, I guess I have never really thought about it, but yes, I do. I trust him completely. I have never had a reason to feel otherwise. May I ask why you wanted to know?"

Jenni pointed up toward Mike. "Your dad and I had an interesting conversation this morning..."

"I hope not about me," Jo's eyes widened.

"No, no," Jenni reassured her. "It was about me. I guess I have huge trust issues because someone I cared deeply about, my ex-husband actually, violated that trust. I'm finding it really hard to move past that."

Jo nodded slowly. "I can see why that could happen. We allow ourselves to be so vulnerable when we trust so completely. Thankfully, that's never been an issue for me and Dare. But then, we're just old buddies, anyway."

Jenni looked to see if Jo was joking, but she saw that the younger woman was very serious. Jenni said nothing but thought, *She has no idea how in love they really are.*

Not wanting her silence to be misinterpreted, Jenni quickly said, "Thanks for that," and changing the subject, pointed to the Hatteras fleet now returning from a long day on the water.

"It's something to see, isn't it?" Jo said. "Especially on the Fourth of July holiday with all the flags and whatnot. What will y'all be doing tomorrow?"

Jenni looked over at Caitlin who had picked up on the tail end of the conversation.

"Well..." she stretched out that one word, looking carefully at Jenni. "Andrew has some other friends who happen to be here on the island, so he's visiting with them for the first part of the day. So... I thought we could take an early ferry to Ocracoke, just hang around a little bit, maybe catch lunch and head back. We'd be in Frisco way before the fireworks. Doesn't that sound like fun?"

"Um," said Jenni. "I swear. What is it about you and early mornings? But I haven't been to Ocracoke in forever, I mean, since I was a kid. But won't there be a huge ferry line?"

"Not if we go super early," said Caitlin who clearly had

this all planned. "And most people who want to be there are already there. Plus, it's a holiday, so no big delivery trucks to contend with."

Jo looked at Jenni and started to laugh. "I'd say that's a done deal."

Jenni and Caitlin laughed as well. They were almost back to the docks now, and traffic was moving much more slowly. Jenni started to add something about Caitlin happily running her life when she caught her breath.

Once again, she could have sworn she saw Caleb in a boat passing them by.

She was seriously starting to question her sanity.

It looked like just guys in the boat, and Jenni felt an uncontrollable sense of relief.

What if it had been Caleb and there had been a woman on his arms?

This constant Caleb obsession was beginning to worry her.

"What is it?" asked Caitlin. "You look funny."

"Oh, it's nothing," swallowed Jenni. "Nothing at all."

Chapter Twenty-One

Not for the first time on Hatteras Island, Jenni found herself waking up with the dawn just beginning to spread its pink and lavender light over the horizon. She grabbed a robe and stumbled into the kitchen where Caitlin shushed her and handed her a cup of coffee.

"Don't want to wake up the others," she whispered. "We can get another coffee down at the ferry dock. How long will it take you to get ready?"

"Not long at all," said Jenni very quietly as she enjoyed her first sip. "This stuff is my elixir."

Then realizing Caitlin wanted more of an answer, she

added, "I showered last night, so I'll just get changed, and we'll be ready to go."

"Sounds good. I'll just meet you outside in about fifteen," Caitlin said.

"Let's take my car," suggested Jenni. "It's a bit smaller, and that way, we won't take up as much room on the ferry. I don't think we'll have many issues going over, but we sure want to get back without any problems."

"Good idea," Caitlin nodded, setting her cup in the sink. "See you in a few."

Jenni added her cup to the pile of cups and wine glasses from the previous night and headed quickly to her room. They all had enjoyed sharing their experiences on the SeaAnna II yesterday evening, and Scott and Barb seemed intensely happy that they had had such a great day.

"That was a truly special experience," Barb had said to Andrew, Caitlin, and Jenni. "Dare is already considered to be one of the finest young boat captains in the Hatteras fleet. I don't think he would have many vacancies on his boat for this summer, so your timing was lucky for sure."

Scott readily agreed. "I have to admit I'm a bit jealous, Andrew. Catching a tuna is a bucket list item for me as well."

Andrew had suggested the two of them try to make up a charter sometime, and Scott practically pounded his soon-to-be son-in-law on the back. "That's a great idea." He laughed. "I like how you think."

The rest of the evening had passed by pleasantly and quickly, and Jenni almost felt herself relaxing except that, every once in a while, she'd have a fleeting thought of Caleb.

She thought she saw Caitlin look at her as if she knew what was in Jenni's mind, so Jenni made sure to always jump into the conversation quickly and either add something or change the subject. She did not want there to be a lull where Caitlin would ask her questions she didn't want to answer.

The truth was, she was often asking herself questions for which she didn't have an answer.

She checked the time as she walked out to her car. It was just after 5:30. They'd have plenty of time to get to the dock and grab that coffee before boarding. She hoped Caitlin was right about the holiday being a slow day, at least at this ungodly hour. Sure enough, as they pulled into the line, there were only a handful of cars ahead of them. That was the good news. The bad news was that the little snack and coffee shack didn't open until 6.

"I'm sorry," Caitlin said. "But I promise you when we get to Ocracoke Village things will be open. We'll have coffee and a good breakfast."

Boarding commenced almost as soon as they had taken their place in line, and before Jenni knew it, they were moving away from the docks. For the second time in two days, Jenni was back in the channel heading across Hatteras Inlet, only today she was seeing it from the ferry's perspective. She could see charter boats ahead and behind in the line, and marveled at the endurance of the captains and their mates who did this work day in and day out all summer long with few if any breaks unless there was really bad weather.

She and Caitlin had gotten out of the car and were standing by the railing, watching the sun as it climbed in the sky, trying to catch a bit of breeze as they moved along.

"I remember as a kid you could get across the inlet in about 45 minutes," said Caitlin. "Now it's over an hour. But people love to visit Ocracoke. The number of day trippers is really crazy when you consider the population of the village."

Jenni thought back to the few trips she and her family had made in her childhood. She didn't remember much except that she was sure she had seen ponies there.

"Hey," she suddenly blurted out to Caitlin. "Are there still ponies on Ocracoke?"

Caitlin laughed as she shielded her eyes from the sun, which, even with sunglasses, was intensely bright as it rose. "Yep. They've got a nice parking area there, and usually, you can walk up on the viewing platform to see them. We can do that if you want to before we drive on into the village."

Which is exactly what they did after disembarking.

Jenni enjoyed driving along the thin stretch of highway the thirteen miles or so into the picturesque little harbor. The ponies had indeed been out, and she took a number of photos, experimenting with her phone camera to see what she'd get.

As they got closer to the village, she asked Caitlin about breakfast spots, and they opted for a food truck that had become rather famous in recent years. "As long as they have coffee, I'm good," remarked Jenni as they parked. "But that ferry ride made me pretty hungry."

"I don't know what it is about salt air," said Caitlin. "But when I'm on the Outer Banks, I am constantly hungry."

They ordered, found a place in the shade, and planned their day.

"We probably should get back on the ferry no later than one-thirty," calculated Caitlin. "That means getting back to Frisco at about three. We won't leave for the fireworks in Avon until eight or so, but Mom expects us for her big July Fourth picnic extravaganza at the house and..."

"I know, I know," laughed Jenni, draining her second cup. "We can't be late."

Jenni wondered how they would fill up the time, but she actually found the hours passing quickly with plenty to see and do.

They found a bike rental place on Silver Lake and decided to see the village that way. Walking would have just been unbearably hot, so they at least got a bit of breeze from the bikes. They window-shopped, visited the lighthouse, wandered down a number of twisting and turning back streets, and just enjoyed watching the boats resting in the harbor.

"The sailboats are incredible," enthused Jenni. "Can you imagine owning one or possibly living on one? That must be amazing."

Caitlin nodded. "We have a friend who does sunset tours in Charleston. As you might imagine, he stays absolutely booked up in the summer, but sometimes in the early spring or later in the fall we can go out with him and his wife. Andrew and I have often talked about saving up to buy a boat someday."

Jenni looked at her friend and felt immensely happy for her. To have a shared vision for the future with the person you love, that's an aspiration Jenni also hoped to have someday. But right now, she felt her future in the area of love was rather bleak.

Chapter Twenty-Two

"Hey, I see a shadow on your face," remarked Caitlin as they turned around in the big parking lot by the ferry docks for the boats that travel to the mainland.

Jenni was often amazed by Caitlin's ability to read her so well. "We have really used up the time. I suggest we return the bikes and try to grab lunch before the crowds really start waking up and getting hungry. We've been lucky so far, but I don't want to push our luck."

It was only 11:30, but Jenni saw the wisdom in Caitlin's suggestion. As they walked up to the one very, very popular harbor side eatery, a small line had already formed. They managed to get seated by noon and ended up eating rather quickly in order to get back on the road a few minutes before 1:00 for the 1:30 ferry departure.

"Once again your planning skills are impeccable," Jenni admitted as she drove onto the ferry, one of the last cars to get on. "We almost ended up having to wait another hour, and in this heat, I'm sure I'd melt."

She waited until they began moving and then immediately hopped out of the car. "I have to have air, so I'm going over by the railing."

Caitlin looked up from her phone. She was obviously texting Andrew. "I'll be with you in a few. Got to keep up with my man, you know."

Jenni rearranged her hair off her shoulders and into a ponytail. She stuck her head in her ball cap and pulled her hair out the back. The bit of a breeze on her neck made her feel much cooler, and she immediately was lost in thought.

She was watching the docks recede in the distance when she felt a tap on her shoulder. Thinking it was Caitlin, she spun around and asked, "Well, how is he?"

It wasn't Caitlin. It was Caleb Prescott.

"Jenni?" he asked. It seemed an odd question since he had obviously seen her first. "I guess I wasn't sure it was really you."

Jenni looked back at Caleb, with a mixture of shock and disbelief.

Then they both began to speak, almost in unison, "What are you doing here?"

They both started to answer, so Caleb stopped and said, "You first."

Jenni's emotions were a mess.

She finally got the answer to her prayers. She was

talking to him. Alone. But she was uncertain about what exactly she wanted to say.

No sense ripping him apart for the gala. He didn't deserve that.

So, she simply answered his question.

"I'm visiting my friend Caitlin at her parents' place. You remember Caitlin. She just got engaged, and her fiancée is here too. They surprised me with the news." Jenni's mouth felt dry.

She wanted to talk to him, but she wanted him to disappear. She was still angry about the infamous "plus-one." How dare he just appear like a magician?

She kept her composure.

"And…" asked Caleb, waiting for her to continue.

"And he's been visiting with some friends of his, this morning and early afternoon, so Caitlin thought it'd be fun to zip over to Ocracoke for a few hours. We need to get back for her mom's big holiday picnic. And you?"

"Strange, I did almost the same thing," he said as he mopped some perspiration from his forehead. "I haven't seen that place since I was a kid, and I thought earlier today might be a good chance to, as you say, zip over and back. I've been at my buddy's place in Frisco, 'The Tackle Box.' It's where we stay for the tournaments."

They looked at each other, and there was an awkward silence.

"Look, Jenni," Caleb began. "I tried to text you a couple of times after your event. Did you even read what I had to say? It was a great time. It was so successful. And my cousin really wanted to meet you."

Jenni was taken aback. She hadn't read any of his texts. She just deleted them when she saw his name. She couldn't pretend that she had. But did he just say *cousin*?

"Cousin?" she repeated out loud. "I had no idea. She seemed so, well, so friendly with you."

Caleb looked at her carefully, and then it dawned on him. "You thought she was my date!" he exclaimed. He wiped his forehead again. "She's my first cousin. We grew up practically next door to one another when she still lived in Raleigh. She's like a sister. She's beautiful and crazy and she's an influencer on social media."

Jenni stood there dumbfounded. "An influencer?" She was starting to feel very foolish yet again.

"You know what an influencer is. Her name is Lacey Prescott. Look her up. She's got a gazillion followers, and she wanted to give *Raleigh Wins* a big shout-out. I thought it would be alright, but I wanted to check with you first," he said, then paused for a moment. "Unfortunately, I never heard back."

Jenni's shoulders sagged. She didn't know what to say.

But he wasn't finished. "We tried to see you after the event, but you disappeared. She had a very early morning flight to catch to New York City, and she insisted we get her back to her hotel. She allowed me to wait for a few minutes, and then she just about dragged me out the door. I told Tory to let you know I wanted to see you."

Jenni took a deep breath.

"Caleb, I guess I owe you an apology," she began. "I just assumed she was your girlfriend. I mean, she was very familiar with you, but now I understand that. I made a big mistake. I'm sorry."

Caleb looked at her for a long time. Behind him, she could see Caitlin walk toward her, stop, and beat a hasty retreat when she realized that Caleb had somehow made an appearance on the ferry.

"Let me ask you something clse, Jenni," he said. "Was I

seeing things? Or was that you out offshore fishing yesterday?"

Jenni nodded yes.

At least my eyes weren't playing tricks on me, she thought.

"I thought I saw you too," she admitted. "But I convinced myself I was the one seeing things."

She realized she had just given away the fact that she thought of him more than her lack of responding to his texts might have implied. She looked away for a moment and then looked back at Caleb. He was frowning.

"I accept your apology for ignoring my texts," he began seriously. "But I think it will take a bit more than that for me to completely forgive you."

Jenni's eyes widened. She thought being sorry would be enough. Then she saw him grinning.

"I know this is very last minute, but I'm leaving tomorrow morning as I have something I have to do this weekend," he said quickly. "And I'm doing the fireworks thing tonight as well. But do you think we could maybe get an ice cream after your picnic and before everyone leaves for Avon?"

"I guess so," she said. "I'm not sure where your cottage is, but since we're both in Frisco, it wouldn't be hard to come back here to that little place on the docks."

"Good idea," he agreed. "And I think there's a walkway out to the beach we could check out. How about I meet you at five-thirty?"

Chapter Twenty-Three

Jenni thought ice cream sounded interesting. But by accepting his invitation, was she opening up another can of worms? She was thrilled with the invitation but very frightened about where this might all end up. With a big hurt for her, no doubt. She was about to decline when she heard Caitlin behind her, apparently deciding she wanted to hear what was going on after all. So, it was Caitlin who said, "I think that would work perfectly, Caleb. We'll be done eating by then, and I'll personally excuse Jenni from clean-up."

Jenni gaped at her friend. "Thanks, Mom," she said,

trying to find her footing in the conversation. "OK, Caleb. I'll see you then. I'm glad we got all that confusion cleared up. My bad for sure."

"I'm glad too, Jenni," he said as he began to walk away. "I'd better rejoin my friend who came along with me. He'll think I fell overboard."

He wove his way through the cars, trucks, and campers and then he was gone.

Caitlin looked carefully at Jenni. "Wow, talk about coincidences. I swear you two have some kind of connection."

Jenni wasn't sure what to say. She had thought about Caleb for weeks, feeling resentful, jealous, and angry about his "girlfriend," but also guilty that she had pushed him away.

Now they had an ice cream date, whatever that was.

Why was she feeling conflicted?

She stayed lost in thought for the rest of the ferry ride and all the way back to "Mermaid's Mansion." She tried hard to engage in the fun and conversation around the table. As always Barb had outdone herself in the food department.

Caitlin could hardly wait to tell her mom about Caleb being back on the island.

"Jenni, I'd say he's a bit interested in you," Barb said, dishing out more potato salad. "I say go and enjoy the ice cream. And don't think about anything else."

Dinner coming to an end, Jenni excused herself to go inside and take a quick shower before heading back to Hatteras.

She had planned to wear white shorts and a cute red and blue top for the fireworks along with some starry earrings, but she wondered if that might be a bit over the top. Then she shrugged and decided she wasn't going to overthink things. She'd wear what she wanted. It was a holiday.

It was still unbearably hot at 5:30 when she got to the parking area by the little snack. She saw Caleb getting out of his car, so she waved, and they caught up and walked to the counter to order.

"I'd normally get a cone," he admitted. "I'm an ice-cream freak. And kind of a purist when it comes to cones. But I'm going to get a cup because I am sure it's all going to melt before I can finish it."

"That's a really good idea," Jenni agreed. They ordered and then, cups in hand, they began to walk down toward the ramp that led out onto the beach.

They talked about growing up in Raleigh and how they had both decided to go out of state for college and how they ended up back where they started.

Jenni decided this definitely felt good.

Chapter Twenty-Four

"I was on a tennis scholarship," said Jenni. "It was strange being away from Raleigh and in South Carolina. But Caitlin was such a wonderful roommate. She played too. We've just always been close, even if we don't see each other much anymore. Although this year, it's been twice in a few months. I moved back home to Raleigh after my divorce."

"You know, I can play a mean game of tennis." Caleb grinned. "Maybe we should make a tennis date."

Jenni felt herself relax for the first time in weeks, maybe

months. "Are you sure of that? Because Caitlin will tell you I play hard, and I play to win."

Caleb laughed. "I played a lot in high school. I wanted to play in college, but there were too many other demands on my time. My parents had great expectations for my schooling, and I didn't feel I could let them down. Lots of pressure, you know?"

Jenni nodded. She remembered how she struggled to maintain her grades and keep playing tennis. "I do know. That tennis scholarship was a big deal for my family–not having to pay for my tuition. I just couldn't let them down. I squeaked by in high school, so tennis was my pathway to success. I was glad I could go to college."

Jenni was surprised that they actually seemed to have things in common.

Caleb looked at her. "My grandfather went to Virginia. I chose not to go for undergrad, but I was offered a great opportunity there for grad school, which I really was excited about. And that's where I met the guys. You remember Jonah, Bertie, and Lyle. In fact, I'm leaving in the morning so that I can get back for Bertie's wedding on Saturday. I'm the best man."

Jenni had rolled her eyes at the mention of his three friends.

"You don't have a high opinion of them, do you?" he asked.

She remained silent.

"You know, since you haven't really met them, that's being a bit judgmental, don't you think? They are really good guys. Just because they're rowdy at a fishing tournament doesn't mean they're not good people. You seem to make snap decisions about a lot of things."

Jenni was stung.

Yes, she probably did. She'd been hurt before, and she wasn't going to let it happen again. All men needed to prove themselves worthy in her eyes. It was a matter of trust, or better said, a lack of it.

Her thoughts flashed back to her conversation the day before with Mike Leonard.

"Well, I have my reasons." She stopped and crossed her arms in front of her as if to protect her from any further verbal assaults.

He stopped too and faced her.

"My ex-husband and I, we were college sweethearts. His name was, or rather still is, Compton Lee Satterwaite the third. Better known as Compy. He's the scion of a wealthy and influential Columbia family. He was also incredibly handsome and bright."

"Go on," said Caleb.

"I fell in love right away. From the moment we met, he was my world."

Jenni took a breath. She felt a breeze and it gave her a chill. "When I went to college, this wasn't me at all. I was a fun-loving, easy-going girl. I loved life."

God, where had that Jenni gone?

"I guess I molded myself into the kind of southern wife that he, and his family, would expect, and I lost myself in the process."

Caleb said nothing, so she continued.

"I graduated with a degree in business, but it was his law degree that really mattered. I ended up having a life of social events like football tailgates and garden parties and weekends at the coast. They were fun, but..."

"But what?" he asked.

She felt his eyes on her, and she knew he was paying close attention.

"I don't know. I guess I never felt like I belonged or like I fit in. But when I tried to talk to him, he was always too busy to listen, or he told me I had it made. That I needed to make myself happy. That my happiness wasn't his responsibility."

Caleb started to say something, then stopped.

Jenni wanted to end the conversation right there but knew she had to finish her story. Maybe by finally telling it in this way, she could rid herself of her demons.

"Perhaps it was my unhappiness that pushed him away, but I felt like the life I was living was a lie." Jenni sighed and looked at Caleb who was gazing at her with a look that made her want to squirm. Too intense. Too focused.

This was not a good story and now he'd know that she was not enough.

She turned and started walking again.

He followed.

She continued the story, needing him to understand her reasons.

"Compy came home from work later and later and made more excuses for why we couldn't do things together. So, perhaps it shouldn't have been a surprise when he announced he wanted a divorce. What was a surprise was when it became apparent that the one good friend I thought I'd made in his law firm was the reason for the divorce."

She took one more deep breath.

He waited.

"Caleb, I was hurt badly in my divorce," Jenni said in as calm a voice as she could muster. "Yes, it's been over a year, but I still carry that hurt with me."

"I can see that," Caleb said somewhat coolly. "You wear it like a badge of honor."

"That's not fair," exclaimed Jenni. "You don't know how it felt."

They'd been walking side by side but now Caleb drew back and faced her. "So, do you honestly think you're the only person who's ever been hurt? It takes work to get over it, but you have to try. I was engaged a few years ago. I loved my fiancé. I thought she loved me. We were planning a wedding."

Caleb's voice had escalated up a few notches, and Jenni could feel people starting to stare.

"What did you do wrong?" Jenni asked.

Caleb's expression went stone cold.

Jenni knew in a moment she'd said the wrong thing, but there was no way to take it back now.

"What did *I* do wrong?" Caleb repeated.

His eyes now appeared sad as he shook his head. "I can't believe you'd assume that it had to be my transgression, something I did, that ended the relationship. That only a man could hurt a woman and not the other way around. For your information it was Esme. She crossed a line that meant we could no longer be together. It doesn't matter what it was, just believe me when I say that I had never felt so betrayed in my life."

There was nothing for Jenni to add. Another "I'm sorry"? That seemed weak and inept. She was fumbling for words when Caleb turned to walk away.

"You know, Jenni, I think you might need to get some help to work through your feelings. To heal. To trust. It seems to me you could have a great future ahead of you, but you'd rather wallow in the past and never allow anyone inside your little bubble of hurt. It's not easy, but that's something I had to do myself. I suggest you think about it."

He walked up the ramp.

Jenni stood there, frozen to the spot.

How had this gone so wrong?

She wanted to call out to him, but she didn't. She watched as he disappeared out of view for the second time that day. This time she felt it would be forever.

Chapter Twenty-Five

The drive back to Raleigh seemed to go on forever. Hot, tired, and drained, Jenni had done some serious soul-searching while finding herself in the heavy traffic leaving the coast after the Independence Day holiday.

She wasn't at all certain about what she needed to do to make changes in her life, but she now was convinced she needed to do something.

She and Caitlin had had several long conversations after her debacle with Caleb, and she'd also taken several long solo walks on the beach in an effort to come to terms with her fears and her feelings.

She couldn't understand why she cared about Caleb so much but just couldn't seem to get rid of her insecurities and her fears.

She was hurting in the same way that she'd hurt with Compy, but she despised her ex-husband.

If she was being completely honest with herself, she knew that she had more than just passing feelings for Caleb.

Still, she hurt either way, so what good was it to try to love someone?

By the time she reached her apartment, she had resolved to do two things. The first was to pay a visit to her Uncle Ron and tell him all about her offshore fishing adventures. The thought of that visit made her feel a bit lighter.

She was very fond of her uncle who was her dad's oldest brother. With no children of his own and his wife, her Aunt Lenore, gone some ten years now, he no doubt was lonesome for family.

She'd been remiss in not visiting him more often.

The second thing was to put Compy and Caleb both out of her mind.

Compy was the past and she had to accept that. He had caused her more pain than she'd ever felt in her life, but he was gone now. Nothing would change what had happened there.

And Caleb just brought the whole Compy thing to life. She was simply unable to separate the two.

Crazy maybe, she admitted to herself, but forgetting him too would make her life easier. He might seem different and have his own hurts. But who could tell?

No, forgetting about him was for the best. She would convince herself of that.

She'd focus on other things, she'd stay busy with work and with teaching, and she'd be fine. Those would be her goals between now and the end of the year. She'd surely be able to accomplish them with ease.

It took her about a month to settle on a date with her uncle who, surprisingly to her, was busier than she expected. He couldn't even find a weekend in August that he didn't already have plans for.

In a way, that knowledge put Jenni's mind at ease. At least he wasn't sitting around doing nothing.

They settled on the weekend after Labor Day, and Jenni was looking forward to getting out of Raleigh and heading toward Black Mountain.

As much as she loved the coast, she also had a fondness for the mountains, especially as summer began to wane and fall colors were on the horizon. It would be a bit early for that, she knew, but just the mountain air would be a welcome change. It had been stifling in Raleigh ever since she'd returned from the Outer Banks.

She was busy packing when she received a call from Caitlin. She assumed it would be more wedding discussions as that had been the major topic of conversation over the past month.

"Hey CayCay," she said as she picked up her phone. "I looked over all those color swatches, and I really think I like the sky blue the best. But I could be happy with any of the others."

"Um, that's good," said Caitlin, sounding a bit distracted. "That seems to be the choice of the other bridesmaids as well, but I wanted to give you the final choice. But that's not why I'm calling."

"Oh," said Jenni, sitting on the edge of her bed next to her suitcase. "What's going on? What's wrong? You and Andrew are OK, right?"

"Oh, nothing wrong with us," Caitlin responded. "It's

just that my Aunt Liz, well, she's never really rebounded from Covid like everyone expected. You know there's the fall fishing tournament coming up and Mom and Aunt May Ellen..."

Jenni fell back on the bed and looked up at the ceiling. She closed her eyes and tried to come up with any kind of excuse, but she also knew it was futile. In a way, she'd actually hoped she could get back to the beach. Jenni wanted to let Caitlin know she was doing fine. She sat up again and completed the sentence for Caitlin.

"And they want to know if I can come and fish again. Be a Reel Southern Lady one more time?"

"Guilty as charged," admitted Caitlin. "But would you? I mean, could you? It would be another long weekend. I wasn't sure of your vacation time and all, but Mom and Aunt May Ellen begged me to check with you, first."

"I'm pretty sure I can get the time off," said Jenni. "I've been handling quite a few things for Dee these past weeks. Her mom just is not doing well, and she wants to spend a lot of time with her. So, I've taken over a couple of her calls and night meetings, and even on a few Saturday mornings. I think she'd be OK with it."

"And you'd be OK to fish again?" Caitlin asked.

Jenni stood up and began pacing around her bedroom. "You know I learned a lot that first time...the hard way. But I'm up for it, I think. At least you won't have to babysit me quite as much. Lord knows I know to flip the bail."

Caitlin laughed. "So true. It's that middle weekend of October, and the fishing is usually really good around then. I'll text you all the details when I get them from Mom, but it will be the same format. If you can come Wednesday and leave Sunday that should cover it."

I'll probably leave on Saturday right after we finish, but they don't have to know that now. No more banquets for me. Then out loud she said, "You know, I'm going to visit my Uncle Ron this weekend. I plan to tell him all about our day offshore with Dare and Jo and everything. But he probably can give me some really good pointers. Who knows, I might show up and be the ringer for the team."

"That would be amazing, I mean, wonderful." Caitlin laughed again. "But thanks for being a good sport. We have all your gear and stuff from the last time, so just check the forecast and dress accordingly. October can be sunny and warm or absolutely blowing and freezing. Oh, Andrew says 'hi' and bye."

"Bye, Caitlin," Jenni said. Now she'd have even more to discuss with Uncle Ron during her visit. She threw a few more things in her overnight bag, set her alarm, and didn't wake up until it went off early the next morning.

Chapter Twenty-Six

There wasn't much traffic heading west on Interstate 40, so the three-and-a-half-hour drive felt much the same as the drive to Hatteras.

Jenni purposefully kept her mind on the scenery she passed and the stories she'd tell her uncle. She had talked to him earlier in the week and said she'd arrive around noon Saturday and leave on Sunday around the same time.

It was just about noon when she pulled into the driveway. Her uncle was sitting on the rocking chair on his porch. He immediately got up, waved, and moved toward her as she got out of her car.

"So good to see you, Jenni," he said as he gave her a huge bear hug. "I can't wait to hear about what you've been up to. You look good."

He grabbed her one bag, led her up onto the porch, and opened the front door for her.

Jenni was struck immediately by the smell of her Aunt Lenore's apple cake. It brought back powerful memories, both of her aunt's as well as her childhood, and she felt tears in her eyes.

"Uncle Ron, that smells exactly like Aunt Lenore's famous apple cake!" Jenni exclaimed, walking toward the source of the wonderful emanation in the kitchen.

"Well, I'm glad you recognize the aroma. I wasn't sure if you would," Ron said.

Jenni looked at him and saw that he was standing proud with a sad smile on his face. "You know, baking her recipes is what keeps me connected to her. I still miss her, but this helps a lot."

This time, it was Jenni who moved toward him and hugged him tightly. "That's so awesome," she said. "I didn't know you could bake."

"I couldn't," her uncle admitted. "But I learned. Have baked my share of mistakes too. But I find it helps me cope, and it actually is very soothing. I share what I make with some of the neighbors and folks at the senior center. They get a big kick out of me...they call me Rolling Pin Ron. But they don't make fun of my goodies!"

Jenni nodded, and she recalled that conversation when they were enjoying a piece of apple cake after they had finished dinner. Her uncle had truly become an excellent cook as well as a wonderful baker.

"You know," Jenni began. "I've been thinking about you and baking and cooking, and in a way, it's like me and fishing. I made some real bone-head mistakes at that tournament this spring, but all in all, I felt pretty relaxed when I was standing there just mesmerized by the waves, the clouds, and the sky. Same when we went offshore in the summer. Catching a fish is really a bonus compared to the fishing experience."

Jenni saw a twinkle in her uncle's eye. "What I think I'm hearing is something I never thought I'd hear." He grinned. "My niece likes fishing."

For the next few hours, Jenni regaled her uncle with her stories starting with her first disastrous cast and the crazy puffer fish to the day on the Gulf Stream. She also shared bits and pieces about her life in Raleigh since Compy and a little about Caleb. Somehow, she found it easier to talk with her uncle than her own parents.

She noticed her uncle seemed to be pondering something.

"Ah, I don't know a lot about these kinds of things, Jenni," her uncle began. "You know if your Aunt Lenore was here, she could guide you better, bein' a woman and all." He glanced over at the framed wedding photo of the two of them from decades ago, and Jenni saw a look of such total love and devotion it made her heart hurt.

"But I can tell you this," he said as he straightened in his chair and looked Jenni in the eye. "We have to learn from our experiences. That's why we have them. We have to do something with them. And then we have to move on."

Jenni found herself wringing her hands in her lap, and she had to intentionally make herself stop. It was clear to her that her uncle had noticed the nervous gesture.

"When I was your age, we never really talked about stress and mental health and all of that stuff, especially not men. But after your aunt died, I really felt lost. I struggled. I admit that now. I talked to some friends at the senior center, and they suggested I see a therapist-type person or counselor or whatever."

Her uncle took a deep breath, and Jenni knew how hard it was for him to share something so personal.

"So, I finally did," he continued, relaxing a bit in his chair. "And guess what? It didn't bring your aunt back, or make me forget her, or any of those things. But it did bring me peace when I learned how to accept what had happened and how best to move forward with the years I have left. I think it was a good thing to do."

"Thanks, Uncle Ron," she said softly.

For the rest of the evening, he shared with her some of his experiences on Hatteras years ago when the big blues ran in late October and November. He talked about his favorite kinds of bait and lures and types of rods and reels. He showed her how he liked to cast. He pulled a huge book on saltwater fish from his bookshelf and together they looked at pictures of everything from the dreaded puffer fish to beautiful, majestic marlin.

When Jenni gave him a farewell hug and kiss on the cheek the next morning, she knew she was leaving with not only a much-improved knowledge of fishing but with a powerful life lesson as well.

"Now, don't be a stranger," he called out as she headed down the driveway. "And let me know how the tournament goes."

She saw him still waving as she pulled out onto the street and realized that this one little overnight visit had given her the strength to do what she should have done months ago.

Chapter Twenty-Seven

That week, she spent her lunch hours researching online counselors. She had decided that given her work schedule and her teaching obligations, it would be easier if she found a therapist online.

Apparently, this was an up-and-coming business model as there were plenty of practices from which to choose.

As she scanned the online reviews, she realized this was something she should have done long ago. Her pride had kept her from seeking help; she always believed she was strong enough to handle anything on her own.

Clearly, that is not the case.

Slowly, she began to feel like she was taking control of her life once again, and that was affirming.

She'd never get Compy back, and she'd probably never see Caleb again, but at least she could move forward.

The thoughts of Caleb made her feel sad once again, and she nearly gave up on the counseling idea, thinking she was too broken to fix. But she kept looking, found a firm that she thought would best meet her needs, and made an appointment online.

She studied them carefully, read reviews, and finally decided on one. She made her first appointment and hoped that she had been wrong thinking getting outside help was not for her.

"Nothing happens overnight," her counselor had advised her. "Work on the little things you can control every day. It's a process."

That first session had been a process for sure. Once she started talking, she couldn't stop.

Her counselor listened, only interrupting occasionally for clarification or to allow Jenni to compose herself.

The tears were flowing freely as she talked both about her failed marriage as well as her issues with Caleb and how conflicted she felt about him.

Over time the tears were less frequent, and Jenni began to understand that a lot of what she had experienced she could have controlled.

At the very least there were plenty of things over which she had no control that she should have let go of.

It was a feeling of relief, and she began to see herself and her options in a new light.

Jenni conceded to herself that she was feeling much better about life in general. She was working on putting Compy and his criticisms and betrayal behind her, and she was also working on not judging everyone by Compy's example, including Caleb.

It was painful at first to realize how unfair she'd been to Caleb, but as her uncle had wisely said, she had to accept, if not quite embrace, each experience, and grow from it.

She thought about texting Caleb to let him know she had finally taken his advice. She typed the text, but at the last minute, she deleted it before she sent it.

If she was going to forget him then that is exactly what she had to do, and sending a text probably wasn't the smartest thing to do. At least in her heart, she knew that she had learned from that painful lesson, and that she was, she hoped, becoming a better, less judgmental, person. Maybe she would even learn to trust again.

It was with that in mind that she accepted a date a few weeks later. She certainly hadn't forgotten Caleb, but she wanted to see if she could function in a normal dating environment again.

Thinking about her fishing experiences, she reminded herself there were plenty of fish in the sea.

She might have lost Caleb, but if this worked out, at least there was a chance for possibility in the future.

Tim Whiteside was a fellow she met while teaching. They went out for a drink with a group after class, and he asked her out for that weekend.

He was bright, engaging, and funny.

Jenni enjoyed herself and made certain that she took him at face value without trying to second-guess what he did or said. But at night, when she was alone with her thoughts, she knew that as nice as Tim was, she didn't feel any chemistry. She wished it could be different, but she also knew chemistry wasn't something you could force.

In her mind, it was either there or it wasn't, and it wasn't with Tim.

The weekend before she left for the tournament, they went out for a lovely dinner. He asked her for her plans for the coming weekend, and she told him she'd be leaving Wednesday afternoon sometime for a fishing tournament. His eyes widened a bit, but then became downcast as Jenni continued.

"Tim, I have to be honest. These past few weeks have been a lot of fun," she said, wringing her dinner napkin under the table. "But I'm not sure this is working for me, and I think maybe tonight should be our last date."

He cleared his throat but then surprised Jenni. "It's OK. I get it. I'm not sure how I feel, but if our being together isn't for you, it's best we figure that out now."

"Wow, thanks for that," responded Jenni. "I thought you'd be all bent out of shape or something."

"I don't come into things with high expectations, or any expectations, really," explained Tim calmly. "You don't know about how something will work out unless you give it a try. You're an interesting and funny woman, Jenni, and I respect and admire you. I sense you're going through some things. I don't know why, I just do. But whatever, you've been honest with me and that's a plus."

They parted on friendly terms. Having decided earlier to drive separately since they lived on the opposite side of town from each other, Jenni sat in her car for quite a while before heading home.

She felt as if a huge weight had been lifted off her shoulders, and not just because of the way Tim had handled things.

She realized she had made real progress over the past

weeks. Maybe, just maybe, she was finally headed in the right direction.

As she pulled out of the parking lot and into traffic, she also knew that next weekend there would be one direction and one direction only for her – east to Hatteras.

Chapter Twenty-Eight

Jenni listened as the last swell of the organ filled the small chapel. She watched as others rose and moved to the rear to pay their respects, but she held back. She wanted to have a few more moments with Dee.

It seemed to have happened very suddenly, although Jenni knew Mrs. Carroll had been failing for a long time.

Dee had apparently been putting up a very brave front, so it came as a shock early in the morning after her last date with Tim when her phone rang, and Dee shared the news. The funeral would be on the following Wednesday morning. All of the arrangements had been in place for some time.

It was just a matter of relatives making the necessary travel plans. Now, as she made her way down the aisle, she thought again about how quickly life passed everyone by. She was so grateful to her Uncle Ron for his wisdom and guidance helping her open up to the possibilities of the life ahead of her.

"Aw, Dee, I'm just so sorry," she said as she hugged her boss and took her hands in hers.

"Are you OK?"

Dee took out a well-worn tissue from her pocket and dabbed at her eyes. "I think I am, Jenni. You know I thought I was prepared for this, but there's no way you can prepare for the finality of it. Somehow, you always think there will be another day."

Jenni nodded solemnly. "You take as much time off as you need. I'm here. I know that we have compassionate leave, and I also know the board will understand if you need more than that."

"My family is here, and we have things to sort out over the next week," Dee said. "But then I need to return to the office. I want to stay busy, and my mom was never one to stay idle for long for any reason, so I'll be back at it."

Dee then introduced Jenni to the members of her family standing in the vestibule. Jenni was about to ask her about her own work schedule when Dee suddenly added, "Jenni, you were great the past two days stepping up and taking care of things at the office in my absence. I've already told the board we're both going to be away for a few days. You've certainly earned your break for the rest of this week. I'll plan to see you on Monday."

"Thanks, Dee," she said with a sigh of relief that she hoped Dee did not notice.

The truth was, Jenni had no idea what she would have said to Barb, May Ellen, and Caitlin if she'd had to cancel her fishing trip. She knew they'd understand, but she didn't want to disappoint them.

Now she didn't have to, and for that, she was extremely grateful.

"When we both get back, we'll have Giving Tuesday to look forward to and the end of the year," Dee was saying as they walked into the very sunny and warm autumn morning. "So, this trip for you comes at a good time. You'll be plenty busy in the weeks ahead."

Jenni hugged her again and headed to her car.

When she checked her phone, she realized she would have time to drive to her apartment and change into something more comfortable for the drive to the Outer Banks. She'd also be arriving a little earlier than expected. She sent a quick text to Caitlin as a heads-up, promising to text again when she got to Whalebone Junction.

She took a moment to double-check the weather forecast but nothing had changed since the last time she'd looked. The entire state was experiencing an unseasonable but not unheard-of warm spell, and along the coast it would be in the mid to upper seventies.

She certainly wouldn't need her hat or gloves, or those awful waders either. She changed into shorts and a T-shirt for the drive, knowing that in October it could just as easily have been raining, with cool temperatures bordering on cold. This would make fishing much more enjoyable. She might even be able to put her feet in the water.

This time on the drive east, she was aware that indeed, autumn was in full swing. Around Raleigh, trees were turning, and many were in their full glory. But the further east she drove, the fewer colorful trees she noticed.

There was such a tremendous difference in the landscape over a relatively short distance.

Jenni acknowledged to herself that she wasn't at all certain she'd like living without a distinctive change of seasons. She was sure the island did change; it would probably just be different.

With the warmth, it almost felt like summer, but there was definitely less traffic than in July. Instead of families on summer vacation, she saw vehicle after vehicle adorned with fishing rods.

This tournament, the "Beat the Drum" event, was the sister tournament to the one in which she'd participated in the spring.

Who on earth comes up with these crazy names?

But at least this name gave her an indication of what she'd be fishing for. What was it Uncle Ron had said about catching drum? And did he say it was different if you fished for puppy drum instead of black drum?

She didn't think so, but she'd ask Barb or May Ellen and follow their lead.

She thought about all she'd learned about fishing since her initiation into the sport back in April. She'd even gone ahead and ordered a few fishing books on her own, some with photos and drawings of fish, and others about the art of fishing.

At least this time around she was much more prepared, which was not hard to do, given in April she'd been absolutely unprepared.

Chapter Twenty-Nine

Jenni made sure to stop at the rest stop and information center at Whalebone to text Caitlin. As she drove toward the new bridge, her thoughts went back to how she'd first met Caleb.

Was it really six months ago?

She allowed herself to wonder if he'd be there with his "Cast of Thousands," all staying at the aptly named "Tackle Box." She had to face the fact that the answer to both those questions was likely a yes. But that didn't mean she would see him, and it was less likely that they would have any opportunity to speak.

She understood now that her tangle of feelings for him had a lot to do with her anger and resentment toward Compy.

Being able to separate the two had been a real breakthrough for her. Jenni knew that she was responsible for what had happened with Caleb, and while that was painful in a different way, at least she owned up to her part in what had happened.

Maybe at least she could say she was sorry if she had the chance. Then again, maybe it was best to keep the past in the past.

Mulling over all those thoughts took her the rest of the way down the island. She saw a number of birds already starting their migration journeys to points further south. The pelicans and the cormorants were species she knew, but obviously, there were others as well. The sea oats were golden in the softer October light as they swayed in the light breeze.

She decided that this was her favorite time of year on the island. Maybe it was all those things she was noticing that made up for the lack of spectacular color that occurred in other parts of the state.

As she approached the entrance to the little subdivision where "Mermaid's Mansion" was located, she was shocked to see smoke rising from the area. She was even more shocked as she saw that a house just two doors away from the "Mansion" had been heavily damaged by what had to have been a very recent fire.

There was still one fire truck on the scene. She assumed it was likely making sure nothing would reignite. A number of people from the nearby cottages were milling around, no doubt discussing the situation.

Barb, Caitlin, and May Ellen were all outside and

underneath their cottage when Jenni pulled in. She immediately jumped out and ran up to them asking, "What in the world happened? Is everyone OK?"

Barb shook her head disconsolately. "Yes and no, Jenni. That house belongs to good friends of Scott's and mine. It's a second home, just like ours," she said, and seemed to be at a loss for words.

May Ellen continued, "Thankfully no one was injured. They had gone up the beach for the day for doctor appointments and errands and such. We'd been in the house all morning consoling Caitlin, so we didn't realize anything was going on until we heard the sirens. Someone on the street had seen the smoke."

Jenni was trying to process everything at once, but something didn't make sense.

"Consoling Caitlin?" she asked, looking closely now at her friend. "I'm not sure I understand."

Barb pulled Caitlin close to her and gave her a hug. "Well, it seems she and Andrew have had a bit of a hiccup. We've tried to tell her that sometimes these things happen, and it's going to be OK. However, we're not making much progress in that regard. We're hoping you can try. May Ellen and I want to spend some time with our neighbors right now to see what they need and what if anything we can do."

May Ellen added, "Thank goodness this village has such a great volunteer fire department. All the villages on this island do, from what I hear. I don't know much about these things, but I think they can salvage most of what they have. The smoke made it look a whole lot worse, not that it wasn't bad enough."

Jenni only half heard what May Ellen was saying. She had walked over to Caitlin and put her arms around her.

"Come on, CayCay, let's go upstairs and have some wine, and you can tell me what's going on. I'm here for you."

Caitlin had obviously been crying. Her eyes were red and puffy. Her shoulders drooped with sadness. But she straightened up and managed to say, "I'm so glad you're here, Jenni. First my news, then this awful fire, and of course, you telling us about Dee's mom passing away. Selfish I know, but I was really afraid you weren't going to make it."

"Hey, I didn't want to let y'all down, but I had no idea about you and Andrew. When did this happen?" Jenni asked as they walked into the living room.

She dumped her bags on the floor and immediately went into the kitchen, grabbed two wine glasses, and found some wine already opened on the counter.

"Right before I left to come here," Caitlin began.

Jenni handed her a glass of wine and she continued, "It started out as just some bickering about the guest list for the wedding. I'm sure we're not the first couple that's had that as an issue. I thought we'd figure it out when I got back, but Andrew wouldn't let it drop."

Jenni knew where this was headed. She and Compy had had similar disagreements, but then she let his mother handle everything and acquiesced to what he wanted. It was easier that way.

Easier then, but looking back, not the best idea. It created a pattern where she gave into everything.

"Look, sweetie," she said, taking a long drink of wine and then placing the glass on a coaster. "I know you're going to think I'm crazy, especially since I'm not the poster child for successful relationships. But it's OK for you to fight a little and hold your ground. It's probably healthy. A strong love like the two of you have can handle this."

Chapter Thirty

Jenni paused before she spoke.

She found herself in a startling position, giving advice to her best friend and wishing that she'd been open to the same thing months ago. Not that Caitlin hadn't tried in her own way, but Jenni hadn't been open to listening.

She felt she had grown tremendously through her counseling sessions. She could see her actions and reactions more clearly now, and she wanted Caitlin to be spared the same mistakes she'd made.

"You mean to tell me you've never really argued before?" she asked.

"Not like this," Caitlin sobbed. "He said maybe we should postpone the wedding, and I was so angry I agreed. But I didn't mean it."

"I doubt if he meant it either," Jenni consoled her friend. "How did you leave things?"

"I guess we didn't," Caitlin replied. "I had already packed, so I just grabbed my things and left. We didn't say 'bye' or 'love you' or anything."

This time, she began almost wailing, and Jenni was at a bit of a loss, but she thought back to her own sessions. Thinking it was better to let her cry, she sat with Caitlin saying nothing.

Eventually, it was Caitlin who spoke.

"I think this wedding stuff has us both on edge," she admitted. "Maybe a few days apart will help us think things through?" She posed it as a question, so Jenni answered.

"I think that's a good way to look at it," she said. "You know my Uncle Ron recently told me that we have to grow from every experience. That's why we have them. I can't imagine a better time to process all of your thoughts than at the tournament. I've come to believe the beach is a cure-all for most everything." Then changing the subject, she looked into the kitchen.

"With all the commotion with the fire and your problems, I'm guessing your mom won't feel like cooking. Why don't we call into Marcie's for take-out and just eat here tonight? I could kill for a shrimp basket."

Caitlin hiccupped and rose from the couch. "That's a good idea. I'll go and splash my face, and I'm sure you want to get freshened up a bit too. I hear Mom and Aunt May Ellen coming up the steps now, so we can tell them a take-out dinner from Marcie's is a done deal."

Surprisingly, Barb didn't fuss at all about not preparing

dinner. It seemed to Jenni that the fire had shaken her to her core, and not having to cook would be a nice respite.

Jenni did inquire as to the wellbeing of her friends, and Barb seemed very relieved to report that, as May Ellen had speculated, the damage looked far worse than it was.

It would take a while to make the repairs, but the couple had already contacted their insurance company and would just stay at their home in Kinston until they could come back to oversee the work that needed to be done.

Barb and the other neighbors would keep an eye on the property in the ensuing weeks.

"That's pretty positive news, all things considered," Jenni said to Caitlin as they got into the car to go and pick up their order. "I have to ask, what were y'all doing under the house when I got there?"

"We were going to hose the house down if we needed to," Caitlin answered and shivered at the thought. "It's been so dry, and you know these houses are all wood. A few sparks would have been a disaster. Thank goodness it didn't get to that."

There was not much Jenni could add, so they drove in silence to Marcie's.

When they pulled into the parking lot, Jenni laughed. "It sure looks like there's a fishing tournament or something. Look at all these rods. I guess with this good weather, everyone decided to show up."

Caitlin agreed as they walked inside. "Great weather for being on the beach in October, but I'm not sure about fishing," she said. "And apparently we're not the only ones thinking take-out."

For a brief moment Jenni thought Caitlin had seen Caleb, and her heart skipped a beat. She scanned the restaurant but saw only two familiar faces, Susan and Chris

Smith. She waved and Chris left Susan to walk over to where she and Caitlin stood in line.

"Welcome back, Jenni," Chris said, shaking her hand. "Nice to see you. And of course, you too, Caitlin. I heard about the fire."

Jenni wasn't surprised Chris knew. Barb had said that the island was truly a small place and news traveled very quickly. But she didn't want to talk about anything too serious with Caitlin's feelings being so close to the surface.

"Are you going to be judging?" Jenni asked.

She had enjoyed watching Chris and Susan walking along from station to station at the last tournament. They were clearly enjoying themselves.

"Not this time," answered Chris, gesturing toward Susan. "That one re-injured an ankle that she hurt back during Hurricane Eva, so she's a bit gimpy. I try to tell her to stay off of it but..."

Jenni and Caitlin smiled.

"Where's the rest of your crew?" Caitlin inquired.

"Well, let's see," Chris thought for a moment. "SeaAnna and Mike are back in Raleigh, closing on their home. They've finally decided to move here full-time. They bought a place not far from ours about a month ago. Jo is going to be tied up with her classwork in Belhaven for the next two days, but I think she's going to try to get here just for Saturday and Sunday. And Dare is still doing a few charters with this nice weather. Won't be long until he's in for the year."

They had been steadily moving up in line and now found themselves collecting their dinner.

"Hopefully, y'all will make it to the banquet," said Caitlin as she prepared to pay Marcie and Jenni picked up the take-out bags.

"I think we will," smiled Chris. "So, we'll see you then. I'll let you go now. I need to make sure Susan doesn't try to get up without her crutches. She's not happy that I'm insisting she use them. Good luck in the tournament. Not sure the drum will like this calm and warm weather, but you never know."

Chris made his way back to the table, and Susan waved as Jenni and Caitlin turned to leave the restaurant. It was crowded and seemed to be getting even more so as they maneuvered back past the line and pushed the door open. Jenni was juggling the bags and almost dropped them as she bumped into someone going in.

"Sorry," she exclaimed, making sure she had everything firmly in hand once again. She looked up and looked right into the face of Caleb Prescott.

Chapter Thirty-One

"Oh my!" exclaimed Barb as she passed around plates for them to use with the take-out. Caitlin had just told Barb and May Ellen about Jenni's unexpected meeting with Caleb. "What on earth did you do?"

Jenni finished the French fry she was enjoying and said, "I looked him in the eye and smiled and wished him well in the tournament. There wasn't much more I could say or do, it was so crowded. I wanted to, but I couldn't."

May Ellen chimed in. "You know there's always the banquet on Saturday evening, Jenni. I'm sure you could find a moment there if you wanted to."

Jenni chewed thoughtfully on another fry. "I want to make amends. I'm not expecting that to lead anywhere, but I really feel that it's important. He only knows me as someone who is clumsy or rude, or both."

Jenni saw Caitlin look up at her, a smile playing on her lips.

"You know how clumsy I am, CayCay, and that's OK. I just don't want him to think of me in a negative light if and when he does think of me. I really wasn't myself the past year."

Jenni looked out into the distance at nothing in particular and added, "I owe him a huge apology."

They finished dinner with no one saying much of anything else.

Barb and May Ellen seemed overwhelmed by the calamity down the street, and Jenni knew Caitlin was thinking about Andrew.

Later, as they enjoyed a glass of wine, Jenni tried to offer her support to her old roommate.

"Caitlin, I just know everything will work out. I think maybe these couple of days will give you both a chance to reflect on the situation and calm down. Absence makes the heart grow fonder and all that. Let's talk about tomorrow now and try to get our minds off this guy stuff."

Caitlin nodded and explained that there was no need to get up extremely early to which Jenni exclaimed, "I can't believe it!" and then laughed.

They decided to have a leisurely morning and head out just to practice some casting in the afternoon. Jenni knew if she felt rusty, her casts would be pretty lame, and she felt very rusty.

With the weather cooperating, that's exactly how they spent Thursday. Barb had said she'd go to the captains' meeting that afternoon and report back that evening on their stations for Friday and Saturday. She also told them she had a pot of chili cooking, and that dinner would be served promptly at 5:30. They promised to be back well in advance, knowing Barb's penchant for being prompt and never late.

Jenni wondered if Andrew had tried to text Caitlin or vice versa, but Caitlin gave no indication either way. Jenni allowed her friend to be alone with her thoughts, while Jenni rehearsed her lines for when she would see Caleb on Saturday night.

Just thinking about him made her feel anxious.

What if he decided not to attend? Even if he didn't show up, she could always call Tory and make an appointment to see him. Still, she knew the banquet was something he and his "Cast of Thousands" really enjoyed.

Thinking about it, she probably needed to be much nicer to them too. Bertie was in all probability married by now, so congratulations were in order.

At dinner that evening, Barb and May Ellen seemed to be in much brighter moods. Jenni found out they'd be fishing on the south beach for the first two stations, and the north beach for Saturday morning. Barb added without prompting that it appeared the "Cast of Thousands" would not be anywhere near them either day. Jenni thanked her for that bit of information and tried to hide her disappointment.

She realized that she was hoping to show him that she was now much more of a real angler and not just an imposter. Honestly, she wanted to impress him.

Friday morning after their usual crack of dawn start, they headed out to the beach. Jenni was far more observant of the myriad types of rods and reels she saw being unpacked, and the jovial mood of the anglers.

Unlike April when most everyone was just trying to stay warm, the gorgeous weather and soaring October temperatures meant there was a lot more conviviality between and among the stations. This would be a very different experience, she was sure.

Learn from it, she heard her Uncle Ron say.

By 5:00 that afternoon, she knew what he meant.

What she learned from the experience of Friday was that sometimes you just don't catch fish. It had been an unbelievably slow day. It seemed her team was doing no better or no worse than any of the others. She heard via the grapevine that some teams caught a few fish, but everyone was hoping Saturday would be an improvement.

However, with no change in the weather, Jenni was not optimistic about their chances. She wondered how Caleb had done, wherever he was, and if he'd been thinking about her.

She even found herself checking for texts, although deep down inside she knew it was highly unlikely she'd receive one.

"Today was very, um, different," she said to Caitlin, Barb, and May Ellen at dinner.

They were enjoying more of the chili from the day before. Barb had made enough to last a week, Jenni was certain.

"Yeah, it was," agreed Barb. "But there's always tomorrow, and the urgency of the situation means we might try some new bait or something. I do know one thing, though. Whichever team wins this tournament will have really accomplished something."

Jenni tried to keep the dinner conversation light,

sensing Caitlin was sadder by the hour. But she also knew, just like with her personal situation, Caitlin would have to sort through her feelings on her own.

After dinner, it seemed to be understood that everyone wanted an early night.

Jenni was actually nursing a case of sunburn on her face and shoulders, and she reminded herself to keep her beach bag by her side tomorrow to reapply lotion often. Even though the day had been long and uneventful, it was tiring, and she had no problem falling asleep. There were no dreams at all about fish, or Caleb, or anything else.

Chapter Thirty-Two

Saturday dawned bright and sunny. She had noticed yesterday that hardly anyone had been wearing waders, and it was warm enough for the men to fish shirtless.

She put on an old pair of shorts and a T-shirt which she didn't mind getting dirty. She pulled her hair up, put her old ball cap on, and met everyone in the kitchen as they prepared to leave. She saw the dark circles under Caitlin's eyes and knew that there had been no sleep for her.

"Come on, CayCay," she said, grabbing her coffee mug. "Let's slay 'em today."

But it seemed Saturday would be no more productive

than Friday had been. At least they were located just off Ramp 43, and the north side might bring them a bit more luck.

Jenni tried to content herself with casting and re-baiting her hook on those occasions when she did get a nibble, but all in all, it was a very quiet morning on the beach. She was totally lost in thought when suddenly she heard, and then saw, a commotion a few stations away.

Jenni wasn't sure but she thought she saw someone sprawled out on the sand. Men were hollering for help. Jenni didn't wait to see or hear anymore. In a split second, she grabbed her bag and ran as fast as she could toward the gathering crowd. As she got closer, she could clearly see the figure of a man on the sand, his rod dropped at a strange angle beside him. People were standing around, but everyone seemed paralyzed.

Jenni went into autopilot. She threw her bag upside down as she got on her knees next to the man. She felt for a pulse on his neck and she listened for a breath. Nothing on both counts. She yelled to a bystander, "Call 9-1-1."

"We have," a voice said.

"Then tell them no pulse, no breath, and I'm starting compressions."

Without hesitation, she began to compress the man's chest. She was so grateful that the hot weather had meant he was shirtless, and that he fell on a place where the sand was more or less even and hard-packed.

She found the proper spot and then pushed down on him, arms straight, with all her strength, and felt his ribs crack under the pressure.

She began counting out loud to thirty, and then grabbed the pocket resuscitator that she always kept with her and gave two breaths.

Nothing.

She went through the cycle again.

Still nothing.

She knew she had to keep trying.

No one had stepped in to relieve her, so she had to assume she would be doing this on her own.

She was vaguely aware that someone was saying over and over again, "You have to save him. Please. Save him."

But her concentration was on the count of the compressions and the breaths.

She thought of the song *Stayin' Alive,* and it helped her keep her rhythm.

She had finished the fourth set when she finally detected a faint pulse. She also heard sirens in the distance but coming closer. Rocking back on her heels, she said to the man who'd been screaming, "He has a pulse. Everyone please, stay away. Keep this area open for the ambulance."

She kept checking on the victim's breath and pulse to be sure they were still there. Both were faint but detectable.

It seemed like forever, but it had actually taken the rescue squad just ten minutes to get to them.

As the crew jumped from their vehicle, Jenni quickly told them the situation and how many sets she had done before she detected the pulse.

"OK. That's excellent, we'll take it from here," a young woman said. She and her counterparts were moving the man quickly, and Jenni finally realized that it was a specialized team that worked the beaches. Likely this man would be transferred to an ambulance once they got off the sand.

"I think I cracked his ribs," Jenni added as they worked to move him onto a stretcher and into the back of their vehicle.

"Better cracked ribs than the alternative," a young man said. "He'll be grateful to you in the long run."

They packed up, and in seconds, they were gone.

The victim's fishing teammates seemed in a daze as they too loaded up, apparently planning to follow the ambulance to the closest hospital in Nags Head, about an hour north. People were helping them throw their rods and equipment in the back of their truck.

Then, a man walked up to Jenni. She was fairly certain he was the one who'd been expressing absolute panic.

He was shaking, and his voice cracked as he said, "He's m-m-my oldest brother. He's Joe. I'm Frank. Frank Ritelli. Th-th-thank you. I can't believe this. I can't lose him. His family can't lose him. I think you might have saved him. Oh, my God."

He started to shake and sob. Jenni asked if anyone standing around had some strong coffee. Or anything stronger.

A bystander pulled a flask from the pocket of his jeans and handed it to Frank Ritellli. He took a large gulp.

Jenni put her arm around him.

"He's in expert hands now," she said, hugging the man, and she felt him relax just a bit.

A different set of sirens started wailing in the distance and knew the rescue squad had transferred his brother to an ambulance.

He was on his way to the hospital.

Hopefully, all would be well.

She refused to believe otherwise. "You go on now," she said. "It looks like you're all packed up."

Another man, Jenni guessed another brother given the resemblance to the other two, asked Jenni for her name and number which he quickly typed into his phone. "We'll let you know," he said to Jenni, his voice shaking as well. "Come on, Frank, let's go."

As they headed off down the beach and onto the ramp in their truck, several people walked over to Jenni to shake her hand. People slowly began walking back to their stations.

Chapter Thirty-Three

Jenni became aware that Caitlin was standing almost beside her.

Now she threw her arms around Jenni and sobbed, "Oh, my God, Jenni, I know you teach classes for that and all, but it never really seemed real to me. You were so calm, and you were so, so..." Her voice trailed off. "You saved someone's life. You didn't panic. That's amazing. It's incredible. I am so frickin' proud of you."

Jenni finally collapsed on the sand and sat with her head in her hands.

How in the world had she handled that? And what if

the man didn't survive? Should she have done more? Something different? She felt herself sliding into self-recrimination but something deep inside reminded her that she had done the best she could do–what she had trained for since her teens.

She was still a bit out of breath, and she allowed herself to breathe deeply.

She closed her eyes and sat very still for a few moments. Then she turned to Caitlin and said, "Please help me throw all my stuff in my bag, and let's go back to where we're supposed to be."

Caitlin started gathering the items that were scattered nearby. She picked up the pocket resuscitator and handed it to Jenni and asked, "Do you always carry this?"

Jenni nodded. "I do. It's just part of my training. You don't know how many times I've transferred that thing from bag to bag, but I always have it. I've been taught, and I teach, that you just never know."

Jenni stood for a moment and looked out into the ocean. "I've never actually had to use it before but, well, I'm very glad I had it."

As they walked slowly back to their station, several folks applauded as Jenni walked by, and her face burned red.

She knew what she had done was what she'd trained for. She hoped she'd never have to do it again. She also knew that anyone of the people she passed by could have done it too, had they taken any kind of training.

Maybe what she had done would motivate some folks. She hoped so.

Barb and May Ellen had waited by their vehicle until Jenni returned. They both hugged her intensely, and Jenni saw they were both crying.

"It's OK," she said, trying to calm them down. "Let's

hope Mr. Joe Ritelli, I think that's his name, will be fine." And with that, she took her pole, re-baited the hook, and said, "Let's try to fish and end this tournament on a high note."

They only had an hour or so left to fish.

Barb caught a blue, and Caitlin did as well.

Jenni was distracted and only paid a bit of attention to what her rod was doing.

She noticed she was shaking a bit and just kept trying to breathe slowly and let her adrenaline return to more normal levels.

She couldn't seem to focus on any one thing. Her thoughts were a jumble of worry for the victim, her feelings for Caleb, and her concern for Caitlin.

They were all quiet as they drove back to the cottage. Jenni was pretty sure they hadn't won anything but that seemed unimportant given the events of the morning.

They were just about to the driveway of the "Mansion" when Caitlin hollered out, "It's him. He's here!"

There, parked under the carport, was Andrew.

Caitlin practically flew out of the truck to meet him.

There were plenty of "I'm sorrys" and "I love yous" and on Caitlin's part, plenty of tears. Jenni thought about how sweet a reconciliation with Caleb might have been had she been able to let go of her past.

When things calmed down a bit, Caitlin breathlessly told Andrew about what had transpired.

He shook Jenni's hand and then hugged her. "That's something, Jenni," he said. "Proud of you, girl."

Caitlin told him about all the people who had shook her hand on the beach, and those who had applauded.

Jenni really hadn't realized that. She knew she'd been in

a bit of a daze in the aftermath. Now that it was all behind her, she suddenly felt incredibly drained and exhausted.

Caitlin was still talking. "Andrew, you have to come to the banquet with us. I'm sure everyone will want to congratulate and thank Jenni. The fishing was lousy for sure but this, well, this was the highlight of the tournament."

Jenni didn't quite feel that way, and she certainly didn't feel like going to the banquet now. It was somewhat surreal. "I don't know, CayCay," she began. "I didn't do what I did for any kind of congratulations or glory. It was an emergency. It's just what I was trained to do." She looked at her phone. "And I haven't heard from anyone yet about how he's doing, but I guess realistically it will take a while."

Barb stopped unloading her truck and turned to Jenni. "I think you should come with us, Jenni," she said. "I'm certain you'll have heard something by then, and Caitlin is right. I understand for you this was, well, not routine for sure, but something you've trained for over many, many years. You were there when clearly no one else was. That should be acknowledged."

Jenni looked at the four of them and realized it would be futile to argue. "I am going to take some time to rest, then," Jenni said. "I'm not crazy about going for any sort of acknowledgment, but, after all, I do have some very important personal business to tend to."

Caitlin looked at her friend and nodded. "Yes, Jenni," she said. "Yes, you do."

Chapter Thirty-Four

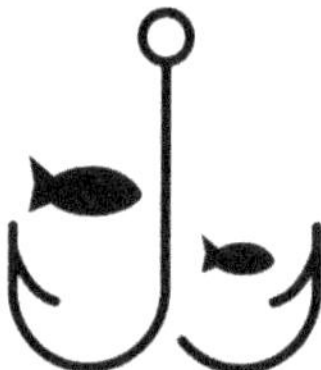

When Jenni stepped out of the shower, she heard a text notification. She was still soaking wet when she grabbed her phone and opened the message. Half-laughing and half-crying, she yelled at the top of her voice, "He's going to be OK!"

She threw on her robe and banged on Caitlin's door across the hallway. "He's going to make it. It's all good," she exclaimed as Caitlin opened the door. "I just got a text from the brother, Frank. Joe Ritelli is at a hospital in, um, let me look again, Chesapeake. He is stable and has regained consciousness."

Caitlin grabbed her friend and jumped up and down. "That is the best news ever," she gushed. "Everyone is going to be so happy."

Jenni added breathlessly, "I guess Frank was able to see him for just a second. Obviously, they will be keeping him and monitoring him closely, but the doctors have said that he should make a full recovery, with a few lifestyle adjustments."

By now the rest of the household had gathered around and heard the news. Barb took Jenni's hand in hers and looked her squarely in the eye.

"Jenni, I know for the past year and a half or so you have considered yourself a failure," she began. "But I hope you've learned that we all have times in our lives where we question our abilities and then something happens to show us just how badly we're needed on this earth. I hope you will remember that."

Jenni considered what Caitlin had said. Before her therapy, she probably, in fact she definitely, wouldn't have believed it, but she could see now that Compy was all wrong for her.

But that didn't mean she was the problem. Like with fishing, she needed to find the right bait and hook to find the right man for her.

She'd let Caleb slip away. She would try to apologize. Then she could heal.

She knew now that all of the flaws in the world weren't hers, and that she could accept herself for what she brought into any relationship. And she could still try to make an effort to impress him when and if she saw him. Maybe he'd notice the change?

Jenni smiled and nodded. Then looking down at her

robe, she said, "So, I guess a robe is not proper fishing tournament banquet attire. Let me finish getting dressed!"

She practically skipped back to her room and then for a moment sat on the edge of the bed and reflected on what had happened that day and what Barb had just said. Then Uncle Ron's voice echoed in her head as well. *Everything's an experience. Grow from it. That's why we have them.*

She knew that the dress code was casual for the banquet. Maybe she would develop a new line of clothing called fishing-tournament casual.

She was pretty sure someone, somewhere probably already had. She had saved a nice pair of jeans just for the event, and she coupled that with a light sweater. It would still be warm this evening but with all of the people attending the banquet, the air conditioning would be on full blast.

She lightly towel-dried her hair, which had pretty much air-dried in the time since she jumped out of the shower. She decided to let it hang loosely.

She was one of the lucky people whose hair had just enough wave, or curl depending on your point of view, to look great without much fuss. She knew she was primping for Caleb, but she didn't care. Tonight, she would make things right.

Once again, though they thought they were arriving early, they could barely find a place to park. Jenni sincerely thought that by now the events of the morning would have receded into the past, but the minute she got out of the car, she knew that wouldn't be the case.

"Hey, aren't you the lady who did CPR on that guy this morning?" a man asked. He had pulled up to park beside them and joined them as they walked toward the entrance of the community center. "I was just a station away on the other side. That's really something, what you did. Have you heard anything about the guy?"

Jenni nodded and said quietly, "Yes, I have. It seems the gentleman is doing well and for now, anyway, it looks like he will be fine."

"Great news," the man said as he shook her hand and walked on ahead. "Best news I've had today. My fishing sure wasn't good news." He laughed and stepped into the hall.

Jenni and her group followed. She was unaware that once she had received the text, Barb contacted Chuck Muller, the tournament organizer, to share the news.

Now people who knew Barb came up to meet Jenni, and those who didn't know Barb soon figured out what was going on and who Jenni was.

Jenni was in the midst of a conversation with an older woman who was sharing her experiences about learning CPR when Chuck Muller approached her.

She excused herself and turned to face Chuck, who introduced himself, thanked her profusely, and then asked her a question. "Jenni, this whole crowd wants to thank you, but if you spoke to each and every one of us, we'd never get out of here. Would you please come to the podium when I introduce you? It will be at the very end. We'll have dinner, announce all the winners, and then I think that would be a good time for folks to show their appreciation."

Jenni was about to decline when she suddenly knew this was a wonderful opportunity. She knew what she had to do.

"I will do that, Mr. Miller, I mean Chuck." She smiled. "But I'd like for you to give me maybe two or three minutes to speak. I'd certainly appreciate that."

"No problem," he said.

Jenni was sure Chuck wondered why anyone would volunteer to speak to a crowd, but at least he didn't say no. She knew people would be anxious to leave at the very end, so she'd keep it short, but she'd make her point.

Chapter Thirty-Five

The dinner line had started to move along.

They went table by table, so Jenni was able to see everyone get in line or sit back down. She scanned the crowd several times for Caleb, but to no avail. He wasn't there.

She nudged Caitlin and asked her to look too, but neither one spotted him. Nor did they see a table where three guys were perhaps waiting for a fourth.

Jenni was crestfallen. She couldn't imagine that he wouldn't come, even if he had no intention of letting her anywhere near him.

She had dreamed of making this apology and maybe even asking him to hear her out. That she had dealt with the demons of her past. Asking him to understand that she was ready to move on now and open her heart.

Jenni had a sharp intake of breath. She realized that what she wanted was to try again with him. But she couldn't say any of that if he wasn't there.

Trying to keep her growing anxiety at bay, she looked around for other familiar faces. The Smith and Leonard families were at the table next to them.

Jenni learned from Chris that Susan's ankle was coming along fine. Susan insisted there had never been anything wrong, and that led to some very good-natured squabbling between the two of them.

Jenni had come to like them a lot. She had heard bits and pieces of their many years apart and then their amazing and coincidental reunion. She felt genuinely happy for them.

Mike and SeaAnna were talking about their move to the beach.

"Jenni, I never thought when I left this island as a young woman that I'd be back," she said, taking Mike's hand in hers. "Or that I'd ever want to come back. Or that Mike would agree. Or that Mike would love fishing so much."

Jenni asked about their new home, and about what it would be like to be a resident now instead of a visitor.

"I guess we'll see," said Mike thoughtfully. "Winter is right around the corner. Maybe I'll help Dare doing off-season stuff with his boat, or maybe Chris and I will just fish." Then he winked. "Whatever it is, I'm sure I'll drive SeaAnna crazy."

That pronouncement caused more laughter.

Jenni saw Dare and Jo make their way to the table.

"Sorry we're late," Jo said, giving her mother and grandmother pecks on the cheek. "Dare actually had a charter today and so he was late cleaning up."

Jenni watched as the two sat down and chatted with Jo's family. She wondered how that relationship would move along in the future.

Jo and Dare seemed so close, and once again she thought that perhaps they had been together for so long they took each other for granted and had no idea how deep their feelings were. *Time will tell,* she mused.

But will time tell for Caleb and me? Is that possible? Will I ever be as happy as they appear to be?

By then it was time for their table to get in line. Jenni craned her neck again to see if she could locate Caleb, but it was clear he wasn't there. She loaded up her plate and thankfully this time she did not trip or fall on her way back to her seat.

The food looked amazing, but suddenly she wasn't so hungry, and she felt her mood begin to slip.

When dinner ended, the names of the winning teams were announced. As Barb had predicted, the winners really had to pull a rabbit out of a hat. Very few fish were caught, and the point spread for all the teams was really tight. It truly was luck in this case that determined the winners.

After the last door prize was announced, Chuck Muller asked the group to remain seated for one more thing. "These past few days might not have been the greatest for fishing," he began. "But this morning something happened that far surpasses anything about fishing. It was about life. I know you all heard about Frank Ritelli collapsing on the beach."

The room was absolutely silent as Chuck continued, "How lucky he was that just a few stations down Jenni Kirk saw what was happening and knew what to do. We got word late this afternoon that he's stable, he's conscious, and that ultimately, he's going to be OK. Jenni Kirk saved his life, and I'd like for her to come up to this podium now so that we can all show her our appreciation for what she did."

Jenni was a bit taken aback by the applause in the room. They were applauding her, for something she had done. This wasn't about her flaws; it was about a tremendous accomplishment. In a flashback she saw how Caleb had encouraged her, even when she'd made mistakes. He always seemed to want to help. She wished he was there to see her step up and speak. To encourage others. The new Jenni. Not perfect but working hard to be the best Jenni she could be.

Chapter Thirty-Six

As she approached the front of the room, people were still standing and applauding.

When they finally sat down, she spotted him. He was leaning against the back wall, a sheepish grin on his face, and a bouquet of loose flowers in his hand.

Her heart leaped, and this time she knew Caleb wouldn't see her fail.

"Thank you for all the applause, the handshakes, and the congratulations," she began. "But I want to tell you that any of you could have done what I did. I suspect there are a number of you in this room who would have, had you been nearby. It was just the luck of the draw that I happened to be so close."

Jenni paused and then continued in a passionate voice. "When my dad was a young teen, he saw his friend's father collapse while they were all fishing at a lake. Neither boy knew what to do, and by the time the ambulance got there it was too late. My dad vowed that he would learn CPR and his family would learn. I not only take refresher classes, but I teach classes too. It's very important to me."

She looked out over her audience and knew they were all listening closely. She said firmly, "CPR training is available everywhere in communities all over the country. It's not expensive and it takes just a few hours of your time. Please do me a favor, do the people you love a favor, and get trained. I never thought I would be given the opportunity to share this message and I'm thankful that Chuck said it was OK for me to speak. I don't have anything more to add since I'm between you and the end of this evening. But when you think of this tournament, think about how it might have ended differently. Thank goodness it didn't. Go, take a CPR class. Thanks."

The entire room stood up again, applauded, and then people began to exit. There were plenty of handshakes and pats on the back as folks came up to Jenni.

She tried to be polite to everyone but there was only one person she wanted to see. He was there and she wouldn't let him escape.

She had this chance, she wouldn't fail.

Finally, Caleb came up to her and thrust the flowers into her hands.

"You are amazing, Jenni Kirk," he began. "Those times you said you couldn't meet for a drink because of classes, I thought you were just coming up with an excuse. I never bothered to ask what kind of classes because I thought it was just a ruse. Shame on me."

"Caleb," Jenni said, forgetting everything she'd rehearsed and now just spoke from her heart, "I did have classes. But I also was very uncertain about how I felt about you and maybe equally as important, how I felt about me. I was very rude to you over a long period of time. I'm just thankful you came to this dinner so that I could apologize."

Then she stopped and looked at him, sounding a bit puzzled. "I really didn't see you here. How did I miss you?"

Caleb shook his head and admitted, "I couldn't locate my car keys. You know I always drive, so we didn't have another vehicle to use. I finally found them in my tackle box. Why they were there, I'll never know. You can believe the guys have really given me a hard time."

Jenni smiled, thinking about Jonah, Lyle, and Bertie, and the first time she'd encountered them, and said, "I can only imagine."

"When I finally found the keys and then told them I wanted to stop at the Sunshine Mart to find flowers, they nearly went ballistic." He grinned. "Well, not really, but they called me a few names."

Jenni looked down at the bouquet and spotted a little tag. "Happy Sweetest Day?" she asked.

"Lord, I don't know. Is it?" Caleb laughed. "I just wanted you to have them. I heard what happened, you know how quickly word gets around on this island, and well, I thought I'd buy these flowers. I wanted to give you, I mean us, one more chance. Speaking of that, do you think we could get out of this hall and take a walk somewhere? I don't think any ice cream stands are open, but the ocean is still there, I'm pretty sure."

Jenni glanced over at Caitlin who had quietly moved

away from the table with Andrew, apparently waiting for the outcome of the conversation to determine their next move. Jenni handed her the flowers and whispered, "Please take these back to the 'Mansion.' I'll be along later."

Caitlin nodded and whispered back, "Take your time." Then she and Andrew headed for the hall door.

A thought struck Jenni as they followed. "How will the rest of your buddies get back to your cottage if you have the only vehicle?" She had visions of them walking on the beach while Jonah, Bertie, and Lyle waited for them.

As if reading her thoughts Caleb replied, "We've been fishing down here a long time. We have lots of fishing friends. They caught a ride with someone else. I think they're headed to Marcie's for a few drinks. Apparently, a local group is playing. I think they're called 'Jamie and the Hanks.' Ever hear of them?"

Jenni admitted she hadn't, but as much as she loved local music, some "alone time" on the beach was more of what she had in mind.

They drove back to where they'd tried to walk just a few short months ago.

It was already dark, but the temperature was mild. There was just a sliver of a moon, and the Milky Way was in its full glory, visible to the naked eye.

They walked down the ramp and stood at the edge listening to the waves wash along the shoreline and marveling at the sky.

"You know, Jenni," Caleb said softly, as he took her hand and pulled her close. "There are lots of fish in the sea. Sometimes you cast a wide net. Sometimes you lose the big one. You never know what you'll catch."

"Caleb," Jenni pleaded good-naturedly. "Enough with the fishing analogies."

"Let me finish," he said. "Sometimes you might catch a blow toad, but sometimes, if you're really patient and really lucky, you'll catch the most wonderful woman in the world."

Jenni looked up into his eyes which seemed to reflect the light of all the stars, and said, "Then let me add my little fishing wisdom, Caleb Prescott. You must know by now that I am hooked on you."

He pulled her close and, taking her face in his hands, bent down to her and kissed her, gently at first and then with increasing passion.

And Jenni knew there was no question, the feeling was mutual.

Epilogue

Caitlin and Andrew's wedding was a grand affair the next spring in Charleston, South Carolina.

As a pre-wedding treat, the couple, along with Jenni and Caleb, enjoyed a sunset cruise with Andrew's friend Chad, the owner and Captain of "Holy City Sailing."

Jenni could see why Caitlin was a fan of sailing, and she had no doubt that someday she and Caleb would be enjoying sailing with them in a boat that belonged to the newlyweds.

Jenni and Caleb went back to Hatteras several times in the following year. They kept up with Barb and Scott and learned that not long after Mike and SeaAnna had moved to the island, Chris fell and injured his knee which required surgery. So, SeaAnna was helping Susan take care of Chris in his recovery while Mike, as he said he would, continued to learn more about fishing.

Jo was deep into her studies, and according to what Jenni had read in the St. Adrian's alumni news, was planning on taking a semester to do research on jellyfish in other parts of the world.

Jenni wondered how Dare would feel about that.

His charter business continued to grow by leaps and bounds from what she could gather, and he was becoming somewhat of a legend on the island.

Andrew, Caitlin, Jenni, and Caleb decided to fish as a team in the "Beat the Drum" tournament the next fall.

They couldn't agree on a team name. Caitlin and Jenni said the names the guys picked were a bit too risqué, while the guys thought the names the gals picked were not "fishy" enough. So, they settled on the "Frisco Four."

It was a gorgeous fall morning, completely unlike the year before. Everyone was in a good mood and, word was, the fishing had been fantastic the past week.

Once they started, they began catching fish left and right, and Jenni was totally in the mix. She'd perfected her cast, she remembered to flip the bail, and no blow toads ended up on her hook.

It was at the end of that session, as she, Caitlin, and Andrew began re-packing the car, that Jenni noticed Caleb was spending an inordinate amount of time messing with his tackle box.

"Come on, Caleb," Jenni teased. "No more fishing for this round. I know I caught one more than you, but you'll have to wait for this afternoon to try to beat me."

Caitlin laughed. "Maybe he's looking for that lure that will bring home the big one?"

"No doubt," added Andrew, a smile playing at his mouth.

When Caleb finally seemed to find what he was looking for, he walked over to Jenni, a serious look on his face.

For a moment, she froze, and then she watched in slow motion as he went down on one knee in the sand, opened a tiny box, and presented Jenni with the most gorgeous ring she'd ever seen.

"Jenni, will you..."

He didn't finish because Jenni was already jumping up and down in the sand, screaming "Yes, yes, yes!"

They hugged and kissed and then Jenni hugged Caitlin and they both cried happy best-friend tears.

Andrew shook Caleb's hand and patted him on the back. "That's one hell of a lure for sure, old man." Andrew chuckled.

Suddenly, Jenni wheeled around and looked at Andrew, and then back at Caitlin. "You knew, didn't you?"

Caitlin threw up her arms and laughed, "Guilty as charged. We wanted Caleb to pop the question at the banquet on Saturday, but he insisted it would be right here."

"I had to propose here, and it had to be in the sand," Caleb said later as they toasted the engagement at Marcie's that evening. "After all, it was Hatteras sand that brought us together in the first place. And I'll happily be 'stuck' with her for the rest of my life."

"We may not win this tournament," Jenni beamed. "But I've just won the prize of a lifetime. The best catch of all!"

Acknowledgments

In that I never expected to write a first book, writing the second one was a real surprise! It has been a different kind of experience, and I'm hopeful that the lessons I learned from "Storm Season," both positive and negative, have made this book a better experience for you, the reader.

I knew when I began to develop the plot for "Hooked on You" in my mind, I would need to do some very specific research.

I am very grateful to Rauna Fuller, a long-time and very successful angler here on Hatteras Island for her explanations of the finer points of tournament fishing, especially from a woman's standpoint. She helped me pinpoint what kinds of fish would be found when, as well as what a rookie angler like Jenni might be allowed or not allowed to do during a tournament.

The two tournaments in this book are completely fictitious, but one would find many similarities in the many fine tournaments that are held here. My husband Dave, a one-time president of the renowned Cape Hatteras Anglers Club, also helped guide me through the tricky and highly competitive waters of fishing for prizes.

For the sequence on CPR, I am indebted to the Hatteras Island Rescue Squad.

Dave and I attended a class in preparation for writing that section. It was important to do, not only from the standpoint of writing, but also from a personal standpoint.

I would encourage everyone to take a class and try to keep current.

I especially want to thank Chief Jack Scarborough, Beach Patrol Supervisor Molly Greenwood, and Captain Naaman Ruter for teaching the class and answering all my questions about how to correctly present the scenario in the book.

Any errors with respect to tournament fishing or administering CPR are totally my own.

We are indeed fortunate to have the Rescue Squad as well as the Dare County EMTs ready to assist us in an emergency.

It's also noteworthy to point out that all the villages on the island have solid volunteer fire departments. We are all in very good hands when it comes to emergency services here.

If you are a visitor to the island, please support these organizations when given the opportunity.

The chapters that detail planning and executing a gala event for a non-profit are based on my years serving in development for both the West Cook YMCA and the YMCA of Northern Colorado. There is no "Raleigh Wins," but youth-serving non-profit organizations in your community deserve your support both in terms of volunteerism as well as financially. They do a lot with so little.

I had a great group of beta readers who took a long look at the first draft and made suggestions and comments. They included Dave, N.P. Littleton, Margie Alexander, Barb Taylor, and Paula Cosnek.

My group of advanced readers provided helpful early reviews to get this book up and running.

There would have been no book without the able assistance of Kim Perry who once again worked with me on formatting the manuscript, connected me with my fine content editor Vanda O'Neill, and basically tutored me through another self-publishing adventure. She also designed another wonderful cover that represents the story so well. Her calm demeanor balances my frazzled nature perfectly.

Thank you to all the readers of "Storm Season" who encouraged me to keep on writing. Your support has meant a great deal to me.

Special thanks to Gee Gee Rossell of Buxton Village Books for getting my name out there in the Outer Banks bookselling world and for her constant encouragement, advice, and support. All of the local booksellers have been wonderfully supportive of my efforts.

A few final notes are in order.

I had an Uncle Ron who did indeed love to fish here. Unlike Jenni's dad, my dad loved to fish as well, and he and Uncle Ron along with my Uncle Rich whiled away many summer vacation days together, brothers of the rod and reel.

There really is a "Holy City Sailing" in Charleston captained by Chad Stewart. If you're in the area, take advantage of a sunset cruise.

For all his loving patience while I shut myself up to

write, and for his belief I can do anything if I try, thank you again, Dave. You're my greatest catch.

And lastly, I have tried to fish, I really have. And the very first fish I caught was actually, you guessed it, a blow toad.

About the Author

Jan Morrow Dawson began visiting the Outer Banks with her family in 1964. She has had previous careers in marketing and public relations, in broadcast journalism, and in the non-profit sector through the local, national and international YMCA movements. In 2005 she did humanitarian work in Kosovo with the United Methodist Committee on Relief. When she returned to Hatteras in 2015 to care for her mother, she reconnected with her old beach boyfriend after a 40-plus year separation and they married in 2016. She spent eight years in the hospitality business at the Cape Hatteras Motel doing everything from laundry to handling the front desk to social media. Now both retired from the motel business, the Dawsons reside in

Buxton on Hatteras Island in the home her parents built. *Hooked on You* is her second novel following her first release of *Storm Season*.

If you'd like to connect, follow her on Facebook for Outer Banks photos, author updates, and information on upcoming books.

https://www.facebook.com/JanetMDawsonWriter/